THE QUEST BEGINS

Donald opened his eyes and saw Vladimir. He concentrated for a moment. "The chips. You were going to make the chips. Do they work?"

"They work better than I thought they would," Vladimir said. "They seem to block out the person's conscious mind entirely."

"No memories, then," Donald said.

"Yes. No memories for them."

Donald held the small, plastic case in his hand. "Well, Vladimir, thank you."

"Don't thank me, Donald. Just succeed."

Bantam Books by Michael Berlyn

CRYSTAL PHOENIX
THE INTEGRATED MAN

For Michael,
This is one of the last

THE INTEGRATED MAN

MICHAEL BERLYN

copies in existence!

Michael Berlyn
3 December 1983
(it's also one of the last signings!)

THE INTEGRATED MAN
A Bantam Book / December 1980

ISBN 0–553–13999–1

Published simultaneously in the United States and Canada

Bantam Books are published by Bantam Books, Inc. Its trademark, consisting of the words "Bantam Books" and the por-
trayal of a bantam, is Registered in U.S. Patent and Trademark
Office and in other countries. Marca Registrada. Bantam
Books, Inc., 666 Fifth Avenue, New York, New York 10103.

THE
INTEGRATED
MAN

1

The small chip of plastic reached the top of its arc, spun on its axis, and fell into the fleshy, upturned palm of Alexander Franklin Morrison. He shifted the chip with his fingers until it rested on his thumbnail, then snapped it into the air.

The chip was smooth; sixteen square millimeters by two millimeters thick; a relatively small piece of hardware that contained thousands of circuits imprinted on each molecular layer—circuits which served as analogs of human neural pathways.

Alone in the darkened office, Morrison sat in his black, overstuffed easy chair. His suit bunched up—puckers appeared in his vest where the cloth was strained by buttons, seams on his pants stretched at his thighs, and the back of his jacket spread across his shoulders to make him look larger than his two hundred sixty-seven pounds. Heavy, pouting lips pursed around a hand-wrapped cigar formed a smile. His heavy-lidded gray eyes crinkled as he smiled, following the path of the chip as it landed on the floor.

He grunted, removed the cigar from his lips, and pushed himself up. The chair creaked under the strain.

The chip lay unprotected.

"Good-bye, Donald Sherman," he said.

Morrison's heel plunged down, crushing the bit of plastic. What had once been the personality of Donald Sherman was now destroyed. Morrison laughed.

He walked to the sheet of polarized glass which lined the entire west wall and looked at the city below. The multicolored and multilayered tubes, bridges, and spires awakened old feelings in him—feelings that had disappeared ten years ago with the appearance of Donald Sherman. With Sherman gone, the satisfaction of owning planets and people regained its charm, Morrison thought.

He tried to clasp his hands behind his back but found the task too difficult. He felt a twinge of pain in his left shoulder and dropped his arms to his sides. He thought of Helene, realized she should hear the news, and went back to his desk.

Still smiling, he waved a pudgy hand over the inlaid metal plaque on his desktop. The screen on the right edge of the desk lit up with the image of a woman's face. Her blue eyes were cold and expressionless as she awaited his instructions.

"Andra, get me Mrs. Morrison," he said.

2

The young woman did nothing to acknowledge his request: courtesy was inefficient. Morrison could not see her hands move, but he knew she was combing through the communication circuits which wound around the globe like cobwebs of laser light. Two seconds after his request, she completed the circuit to his home.

The screen flashed a random color display while he waited for Helene to accept the call. It took her thirty seconds.

His smile still stretched across his face. He caught a glimpse of the old beauty which lay beneath the restructured face before him—a face which lied to those who knew her age. The wrinkles and excess fatty deposits had been removed.

She looks fifteen, no, twenty years younger, Morrison thought, and it still doesn't help. Beneath that smooth skin lies the same, cold, calculating bitch.

He wondered why he had bothered to call in the first place. What had he been thinking when he decided to share his news? She wouldn't be happy to hear it.

Helene sighed. "You crushed it, didn't you?"

"Yes. He's dead."

She threw back her head and laughed. Morrison saw the deep lines in her neck, the lines the surgeon had missed. He turned red, angry with himself for letting her intimidate him so easily, and then redder as his anger mounted.

"Stop that!" he shouted.

But she was already quieting down. The spasm of laughter died. "You're really something, Alexander," she said, wiping a tear from her youthful right cheek. "You've crushed a chip and now it's over." She wiped a wet finger on her dress.

3

"It *is* over. Sherman is dead. All the murders and destruction will stop now that the miners are without a leader."

She shook her head. "Your stupidity amazes me. How can you be so blind? For a man who controls hundreds of planets—"

He broke the connection shaking with rage. His blood pressure rose and the congestion built in his temples. He sat back and forced himself to relax, resigned to the fact that Helene would never understand, would never change.

But even though his wife had broken his mood, when he turned back to look at the smashed chip on the floor, his smile returned.

Sherman was, at last, dead.

Snowy white.

The beads of dew sparkled, crystallized in the chill of the morning. The ground crunched: frozen blades of grass and mud dotted with ice puddles were crushed beneath his boots.

Donald Sherman stopped for a brief rest, knowing that he should not stop at all. He turned to the north and looked back at the valley behind him. His breath was a ragged stream of pale, white mist, and his feet felt the chill creep in. Hands jammed into jacket pockets and curled into fists, he tried to shake off the cold and wished for the warmth of the morning sun. He turned back to the south.

If they were not already after him, they would not be coming at all. The sun would melt the trail his boots had left in the frost. Although his direction would have been simple to guess, he did not think that anyone left behind was physically capable of following.

The miners in the barracks had smashed the

company's surveillance equipment in the staged riot, and the guards had arrived just when the nerve gas had been released. He allowed himself a smile.

A scar ran from his left cheek down across both lips, ending at his chin, distorting the smile into something ugly, lopsided. His lips cracked.

From behind the distant mountains to his left, the sun rose. It was a red dwarf, and as it topped the mountains, it turned the sky crimson. Clouds passed before it and the sky darkened to a blood-red. His tall, lanky, youthful body cast no shadow and, with each step, his shoulders sagged forward and his long legs ached with fatigue.

The still houses slept in the valley behind him. He knew no smoke rose from the chimneys, no early morning fires warmed the inhabitants, no dogs barked to awaken children for school or play, no men or women rose to prepare for the long day working at the mines a half kilometer to the east. No motion. No activity. No life.

The gas had killed the entire town.

Hopefully, the neighboring village to the east and the supply town to the west had been eliminated, too. If all had gone well, he would have time to walk to the spaceport in safety.

Donald Sherman had the utmost confidence in his selves.

As the sun rose over the mountains behind him, his shadow stretched out like a guide to the spaceport. The early morning sun reminded him of another time, another planet.

The dead village was already being warmed, but no sun could take the chill out of the bodies that lay there with unearthly smiles. As he watched his shadow move in rhythm with his short, stocky, mid-

5

dle-aged body, Sherman smiled. The village had grown in balance with the planet's ecosystems and it would die the same way.

No people would stir from their nice, warm beds, no children would awaken to a day of boredom at the company's day-care center, no coffee cups would appear as if by magic on gleaming plastic breakfast tables. As he walked to the west, toward the spaceport, Sherman thought it was good he left the native bacteria alive.

At least they would have something on which to thrive.

The sun peaked over the mountains and he had to shield his eyes from its direct glare. The cold hurt his thin, delicate hand as he removed it from his coat pocket, but it was little discomfort to suffer compared to those who had died in the supply town's barracks.

Before him the spaceport grew as his long, graceful legs continued their steady pace. The stitch in his left side, far below the woman's breast, caused him some concern. To rest now, though, would make him late.

As he walked, he reached for an imicig, patted his fur coat pocket and realized she probably did not smoke. Walking in a woman's body was different, but he found that if he let his mind wander and did not concentrate at all, the body propelled itself.

He inhaled, waited a moment for the imicig's drug to take effect, then exhaled. His tall, lanky body cast a thin shadow to his right, covering the already melting patches of frost as he continued on his steady pace to the spaceport.

He saw the figure in the west first; they were

equidistant from the spaceport's towering structure, but approaching from right angles. Sherman waved his arm in the prearranged manner; the woman in the distance waved back.

Good, Sherman thought. She made it, too.

Then the west was taken care of, and with no other settlements within a thousand kilometers, only the east remained. The security men from the spaceport had hopefully rushed to help quell the riot in the east village and had left the spaceport unguarded.

He stopped, flicked the imicig a few meters to his left and waited for the little, middle-aged man. He watched the east, squinting against the sun. A few minutes passed before the man appeared.

He waited until the man's limbs were easily discernible and then waved. The little figure returned the wave and Sherman smiled again. He had succeeded.

Now, the spaceport.

The spaceport was not designed for pedestrians. The main entrance was through a set of sliding glass doors which opened onto a roadway ten meters above the ground. It was aesthetically pleasing when approached by public transportation or aircar, but approached on foot, it towered overhead.

The two men and the woman met beneath the ramp's discolored, concrete forms. Sherman felt a mild discomfort, like an itch in the back of his mind. Anxiety, he realized. After having made the trek overland with nothing but a few clouds overhead, the presence of the roadway above was unnerving.

As if on cue, the three people shifted their weight from the left foot to the right, jammed their hands deeper into their pockets, and looked at each other. The short, stocky man sniffled. The tall, lanky man with the scar on his cheek cleared his throat.

"Any problems?" he asked.

The woman and little man shook their heads.

"Good," the tall one said. "I don't expect to need either of you for a while. I'll insert you if and when the opportunity for updating arises. We're on to Lanta 2. Any questions?" he asked, knowing there would be none.

They had already removed their coats and unbuttoned the top button on their work shirts, turning their backs to him. In the back of their necks, directly below the base of their skulls, was a thin metal slot. Protruding from the slot was the edge of a thin piece of plastic. Sherman stepped forward and removed the white chip from the woman. He reached into his jacket pocket with his free hand and withdrew a small, plastic case. It snapped open with a slight pressure from his thumb. He carefully placed the white chip from the woman, then the white chip from the man into the foam-lined recesses next to a red chip. Two recesses were empty.

The two people refastened their clothing and turned to face him.

"How did it go?" the woman asked evenly.

"Fine," Sherman said.

"No problems at all?" the short, stocky man asked, rubbing his short, bristly hair with a palm. "I mean, it went all right?"

Sherman nodded. The man broke into a baby-faced grin. Sherman looked at them and searched for the right words, the words to express his emotions, but the deeper he dug, the more difficult it was to verbalize what he felt.

"Thank you," he said at last. He hesitated for a moment, shifted his weight, and added, "You don't have to go through with the rest of this if you don't want to."

"My husband and children are dead. Back there," the woman said, pointing to the west. "There's nothing left for me. I don't mind since we've—I mean, you've—succeeded."

The short man nodded in agreement.

They took the capsules from Sherman's outstretched palm and, without hesitation, placed them in their mouths. As the gelatin capsules dissolved, the scarred man climbed the concrete forms to the roadway.

They were dead before he reached the top.

The shuttle was empty but ready as always for passengers. Calming colors of light blue and mint-green housed rows of plush, imitation velvet acceleration seats on each side of the aisle; the false viewports were carefully placed to help relieve and control the potential claustrophobics; the small packages of snacks and amusements were stowed in compartments before each seat. Every aspect of the shuttle was designed in an attempt to make the passengers forget and ignore the thin metal shell that protected them from space. It was a carefully controlled atmosphere planned to erase the impression of danger.

Sherman settled into the seat nearest the door and waited. The only people in the spaceport had been miners, chips inside their receptacles feeding information to them on how to run the semi-automated spaceport. The guards and supervisors had left to help as he had hoped.

It was warm in the ship and he removed his jacket, laying it on the seat next to him. He relaxed when he heard the hum of the artificial gravity system.

All systems on the shuttle were automatic. As the ship rose, holographic scenes flashed onto the viewports to create the feeling of movement and space. Sherman did not bother to look.

He tried not to think of the carnage he was leaving behind. No matter how willing the victims, it had still been mass murder. Three communities deliberately destroyed. He hid his face in his hands and waited for the journey to end.

Of the two remaining planets within the Lanta System, Sherman had chosen the neutral one: Lanta 2.

Bobbi Osaka-Chien was nude, lying on her side. She looked at Morrison's sleeping form. When he had arrived at her door, elated, eager for the attention Helene never gave him, Bobbi had opened her arms. She had taken him in, undressed, massaged, and fed him; after sex, she led him to her bed.

She was used to the luxuries he lavished on her. She earned them by providing him with emotional responses he could not get elsewhere. For this, she was paid well. It was her responsibility to be there when he wanted her.

A chime sounded in the living room and she knew it had awakened him. Morrison opened his bloodshot eyes.

"Who?" he asked, still half asleep.

"Shhh. Go back to sleep. You need your rest," she said in a soft, protective tone.

Morrison grunted and rolled over onto his side. Bobbi eased out of bed and walked into the living room—a room twice the size of most luxury apartments. The ceiling was seven meters high and the room was twenty meters long. She headed directly for the wall where the phonescreen was hidden. She pressed a touchplate; a panel slid down and into the wall to reveal the screen. She touched the monitor button and faced the image of a woman. The woman's tight-lipped smile, functional rather than stylish hair, and freshly scrubbed face contrasted with Bobbi's appearance. It was Morrison's secretary, Andra.

Bobbi knew Andra had strict orders not to disturb Morrison in her apartment unless it was important. She pressed the accept button.

"Mr. Morrison, please," Andra said.

"He's asleep."

"Then wake him."

Bobbi sighed and went back to the bedroom. She leaned over Morrison's sleeping form and caressed his shoulder until he stirred.

"It's your secretary," she said.

He got up quickly, grabbed his silk robe, and pulled it on. He tied the sash and adjusted it while he walked to the screen. As he saw his secretary's face, he noticed the deep lines across her forehead. Morrison nodded.

"Yes, Andra."

"First, Mrs. Morrison already knows everything— she was sitting in your office at home when the message from Lanta 1 came through. She must have pressed the monitor button. As soon as the message was over she was on the circuit and trying to get through to you. She's still holding."

That figures, he thought. I'm surprised she isn't outside the door, pounding on it, trying to break it down. "All right. Let her hold for a few minutes. What happened?"

"Lanta 1. Three communities wiped out. The pattern was a little different, but close enough. They found two bodies at the spaceport."

"Impossible." Morrison's face went white and he felt a sinking feeling in his stomach. "I killed him myself."

11

"According to our field men, someone boarded a shuttle for Lanta 2. The shuttle has already landed and our man who's following is a little over an hour behind him."

Morrison shook with rage and frustration. His face turned deep red and the veins in his neck bulged.

"We still have a chance of catching his trail. Our people have been notified," Andra said. "I'll inform the authorities."

"Please," he said, knowing it would do no good. He silently cursed himself for not buying Lanta 2 when he'd had the chance. Now that it was neutral, an independent planet, there was nothing he could do. "Who's our man there?"

"Walters-Meyer," Andra said.

"Call him personally." He turned and motioned Bobbi out of the phonescreen's range. "And put my wife through."

Andra nodded once and her image dissolved. It was replaced with the image of Helene's face.

"So, he's dead, is he?" she asked.

That's one thing about Helene, he thought. She doesn't waste any time.

A combination of hatred and disgust showed on his face. He knew she reveled in seeing him like this, out of control, and this increased his anger.

"I crushed the chip. He's got to be dead."

"A chip. Can't you see? Other chips must exist. All you did was fulfill a childish fantasy by destroying it. We might have used it." Her eyes were cold. "We could have inserted it into any one of the miners and questioned him."

"He wouldn't have talked."

"He would have. No one stands up to torture."

Bobbi cringed and slowly lowered herself into a chair. Morrison wanted her out of the room—listening to music tapes, watching her goddamned literary

12

holotapes, anything—but for her to get to the doorway, she would have to walk through the screen's line of sight. That wouldn't have done at all. He didn't need to flaunt his relationship with Bobbi.

"He could have told us how many more chips there are," Helene said. "But no, your childish ego demanded satisfaction. I told you it wasn't over. Was it worth—"

Her image vanished as Morrison pressed the button, breaking the connection.

At least she doesn't have this number, he thought. And Andra will never give it to her.

He felt a hand on his arm, startling him, and realized it was Bobbi. She pulled him by the crook of his elbow and led him to the couch. She sat beside him.

"Alex?"

Morrison pushed her away. "Not now, Bobbi. I've got to think."

2

The doorbell chimed.

William and Sandy Carter watched the program on their holoset. She nudged him with her elbow.

"Don't bother me now. They're about to reveal another clue," William said.

Sandy sighed, got up from the couch and walked to the right side of the room. She was small, a full head shorter than William, had blonde hair, and an attractive figure. She enjoyed looking good; that was one of her major reasons for not having children. That, and their economic state. Sandy had seen what had happened to her neighbor, Gloria

Prist-Wells. After three children, Gloria looked ten years older than she actually was.

Sandy peered into the hologram and from that angle, she could see the next clue. It was hidden behind a doric column.

The bells chimed again.

"It's just some gauze," she said.

"Gauze?" William asked. "Where did gauze come from?"

"Don't ask me. Maybe the murderer was a medi-tech." She sat next to William again. "Now that you know the next clue you can answer the door."

"I want to see him discover it. You know that's half the fun."

"Answer the door," she said, sighing.

William got up. On his way through the empty hallway, he took a mental inventory of what was left and what they would probably take. Three days ago it had been the dining room set. They had been very nice about it and had shown William the court order, but they went about their business anyway.

Sandy made enough money from her job for them to get by, but not enough to meet all their payments. William had held a good position with Weather Control, but when the agency shifted to automatic loops, his job had been phased out.

William was 175 centimeters tall, had brown hair and brown eyes. His face radiated strength and stability, an inner patience and control.

He braced himself and opened the door.

A short, slight man dressed in a conservative business suit stood in the doorway. He pushed his glasses up on the bridge of his thin nose and cleared his throat.

"Mr. Carter?"

William nodded.

"Are you busy?"

William nodded again. He barred the way into his apartment and stared stonily at the man. The man removed a handkerchief from an unzipped jacket pocket and wiped the beads of sweat from his forehead. He looked weary.

"My name is Benjamin Douglas, Mr. Carter. Do you think I might come in for a few minutes? That is, if you're not too busy."

"What is it you want?"

"Just to talk."

"I'm not buying anything. I can't afford it," William said, bored with his own standard reply.

"Maybe I should come back when you're not so busy..."

William sighed. "Listen, Mr. Benjamin—"

"That's Douglas. Benjamin Douglas."

"All right, Mr. Douglas. I don't know what your game is, but if you try to sell me anything—anything at all—I'll throw you out."

William stepped aside to let the little man pass, like he had let the countless other salesmen pass. Only after he was in the apartment did William notice the slim, black attache case Douglas carried under his arm.

He's up to something, William thought. I never should have let him in.

He led the man into the kitchen, feeling awkward. The man looked around the kitchen.

"Mind if I sit down?" Douglas asked.

"Well, I don't have much time..."

"I'm not going to try to sell you anything, Mr. Carter. I'm fully aware of your financial position. As a matter of fact, I'm here to rectify it," he said, patting his case.

"Sit down."

16

"Thank you," Douglas said, pulling a chair away from the kitchen table. He swung his attache case up and placed it on the table top. "Is Mrs. Carter at home, too?"

"Yes, but she's busy right now."

"Oh, I see. Perhaps we should wait for her. It's much more difficult if I have to go through the entire presentation twice."

William nodded. "Just who are you?"

"I've already told you my name. Did I give you a card? No? That's terrible. No wonder you're so reticent."

Douglas unzipped a different pocket on his jacket and withdrew a small business card. He presented it to William.

William looked at it. He had seen cards like this before, but not very often. They were expensive and businessmen seldom gave them away. In the center of the card was a hologram of Earth, spinning slowly on its axis. Floating in the black background, at what appeared to be 2.5 centimeters in from the card's surface, was some lettering:

AFM MINING CO. BENJAMIN DOUGLAS, REP.
AFM-7720-X1020

"I think you've got the wrong person," William said, handing back the card.

"No, I don't think so—unless your wife's name isn't Sandy. And keep the card."

What the hell does the Morrison Mining Company want with me? William thought. Maybe it's a job. "Listen, Mr. Douglas, let me get my wife. I'll be right back." He started walking out of the kitchen, then stopped. "You will wait, won't you?"

Douglas nodded. Those cards usually do the trick, thought Benjamin Douglas. He pushed his glasses back onto the bridge of his nose, smiled, and waited for the Carters.

Lanta 2. A neutral, independent planet.

A planet where Interplanetary Monitors could not bother him. A place where he was a free man—not a fugitive.

Sherman remained seated, waiting for the automatic systems to complete their mock sterilization. It was a joke, and everyone knew it, but the Interplanetary Monitors had deemed it necessary to prevent contamination from planet to planet.

He smiled when he thought about it. Almost all of the planets were terraformed, and no matter how well the sterilization worked, he knew that anyone breathing a planet's atmosphere would carry bacteria inside their lungs to a new planet. Contamination was certain. And yet the IM Agency continued their sterilization procedures.

He held his jacket in his lap. He touched the small, plastic case in his pocket and felt reassured. He tried not to think about the trail of destruction he had left on Lanta 1, hoping the image of the dying, smiling miners would fade from his mind.

The hum in the ship stopped and a plaque in the armrest glowed, indicating it was safe to disembark. He stood up and swung the jacket over his shoulder. He turned to his left and waited for the door to open.

No one should be waiting for him outside the shuttle. If Morrison had acted immediately, there would still have been no way he could have had someone there waiting. But Sherman knew that he did not have much time. If any.

Since Lanta 2 was independent, Morrison could take no legal action against him. Morrison could inform the police, but they could not help. Legally. Unless Sherman committed a crime on Lanta 2, or rubbed the head of the planet's police force the wrong way, he was a free man. But Sherman knew better. Morrison would have his men track him down, delay him, or if that proved impossible, kill him. Sherman realized he was anything but safe.

The door slid open, whining, and clanked to a stop.

It was a far more inviting scene than the desolation he had seen on Lanta 1. This planet was Edenic in comparison; lush trees swayed softly in a gentle wind to his right, and as far as he could see there was grass, trees, and rolling hills. To his left was a modern spaceport. It was unassuming, glass and concrete, but still aesthetically appealing.

Sherman descended the stairs. There was a uniformed immigration officer waiting for him.

"Hello," the overweight man said.

Sherman nodded.

"Alone on the shuttle?"

"Yes."

"That's strange. This one's from Lanta 1, isn't it? There's usually at least half a dozen employees coming off to make—"

"Yeah, it was strange," Sherman said. "There was no one at the spaceport, either."

The officer looked at Sherman and scowled at the long scar which ran down his face, the dirty, frayed, weather-beaten clothes, and the emptiness in his dark eyes.

Sherman smiled, but the scar changed it to something else. "Which way do I go to clear?"

The officer pointed to a set of doors behind him.

"Thanks," Sherman said.

He walked past the balding immigration officer, ignoring the feeling that the man was staring at him. Sherman thought the man might be in Morrison's employ and hoped it was only his own fear.

There were people on Lanta 2 who would help him. They would listen to him, understand what he went through, but he remembered all the others squirming when he mentioned the deaths, no matter how they tried to hide it. They could sympathize and empathize, but only to a point.

The doors slid open as he approached them. He saw the lines of people, passengers from newly arrived ships, and stood at the end of a line behind a woman. The line moved quickly.

"Your card, please," said the man behind the counter.

Sherman handed him his identification card.

"And how long do you plan to stay, Mr. Ceros-Livingston?"

Sherman shrugged. "Depends."

"A salesman?"

"Yes."

The man made a mark on a form, nodded, and examined the card. Sherman watched anxiously as the man turned it end over end, rubbing the smooth plastic surface between his finger and thumb.

"Just what do you sell, Mr. Ceros-Livingston?" he asked.

Sherman reached into his jacket and withdrew the small, plastic case. He snapped it open and, holding it in his palm, turned his hand so the man could see the chips. "Learners, Helpers, Specialty Chips—you know." He saw a look of disgust flash across the man's face.

"There is a market for them here, of course. We're an independent planet." He pressed a button to record Sherman's face and identification card. When he had finished, he handed Sherman back his card and gave him a booklet. "Please read this before leaving the terminal, Mr. Ceros-Livingston. Our planet's customs are not that different on a galactic scale, but there are differences. You are subject to all local laws, regulations, customs, mores, as well as those blanket planetary ones which apply," he said in a monotone.

Sherman thanked the man and looked for an exit. He noticed the immigration officer staring at him, arms folded, leaning against a wall. Sherman stared back for a second, memorized the man's features and then walked to the underground tube that would take him to the city of Alsis.

"What does he want?" Sandy asked.

William Carter shrugged. "He said he's not here to sell us anything, and he hasn't repossessed anything. He says he just wants to talk."

Her eyebrows arched upward. "Well, stall him for a few minutes."

"Sandy, you look fine," he said, rubbing his stubbled chin. "Don't worry about it. Let's just go in and see what he wants, okay?"

"Okay," she said grudgingly.

They left the holoset on.

Benjamin Douglas had opened his attache case and was leafing through some papers. He looked up when they entered.

"Ah, you must be Mrs. Carter," Douglas said, rising to his feet and offering his hand.

She kept her arms by her sides and looked the little man up and down. "That's who I am. Who are you?"

"Didn't your husband show you the card?"

William looked like he was going to say something, but Sandy cut him off. "Never mind that. *You* tell me."

Douglas introduced himself.

"And what is it you want?" Sandy asked.

"Sandy," William said harshly.

21

She looked steadily at Douglas. "You must excuse my husband. He is a very trusting person."

Douglas smiled amiably. "A very rare quality in today's society."

"In any," Sandy said.

"Why don't we sit down?" William asked.

Douglas waited for them to be seated and then sat down. "I'm going to cut right to the point, Mr. Carter. I don't usually do this, but I can tell you're both intelligent people, and I can see—"

"The point, Mr. Douglas?" Sandy interrupted.

"Yes, the point," he muttered. "I know you are going through rough times right now. Finances aren't what they should be."

"So?" Sandy said.

"I have a proposition for you. I recruit families for homesteading. You know, the Morrison Mining Company does more than just mine. We have several nice planets that are low in metals, just waiting for people to settle them. You may not see yourselves as recruits right now, but if things don't get better for you, if things should get worse, we would like to have you in our family."

Douglas reached into his case and withdrew a multicolored folder. He handed it to William. William bit his lower lip as he scanned the promotional devices and holograms. They showed a planet, some close-ups of small houses and communities already in operation, the entertainment facilities, and some other buildings William assumed were schools.

Douglas handed Sandy a similar brochure. She glanced through it quickly and handed it back to Douglas.

"No thank you," she said.

"Well, Mrs. Carter, why don't you hold onto the pamphlet? I have plenty—"

"No. And take this one, too," she said, yanking the

22

other from William's grasp. "Just what do you think we are? We may be having a hard time paying all our bills, but it won't stay like this for long. William will find another job."

"I'm sorry you feel that way, Mrs. Carter." He glanced up at William and saw he was still biting his lower lip, staring at the table top.

"We'll get back on our feet, Mr. Douglas. We don't have to homestead to survive. Why bother us? There are millions of people whose financial positions are worse than ours."

Douglas rose from the table and closed his black attache case. He smiled nervously, now anxious to be on his way since the proposal was rejected. He still had several calls to make in the building; there were the Prist-Wells, the Lawson-Frams, and one down in the sublevels, the Newton-Tates. "I'll be going, then. I hope your situation improves," he said, moving toward the doorway.

William stood up. "I'll walk you to the door."

As Benjamin Douglas shook hands with the young man, he saw William nod. The door slid shut and he caught a glimpse of his business card protruding over the edge of William's top pocket.

Douglas smiled. Some people you can't sign on the first visit, he thought. He was glad he would not be there for the argument.

Morrison's ship was big for a private yacht. The staff had their own cabins on the level below his; Andra and Bobbi had staterooms off the same passageway. Helene occupied an adjoining cabin, but they had talked little since boarding.

Morrison sat in the lounge, the ice in his drink already melted. Andra sat on his left, ready to act as his liaison if and when he needed her. The only other person in the lounge was the bartender.

Morrison hated to watch his employees work. The way they ran around trying to look unobtrusive always looked nonproductive to him.

The lounge was circular, the bulkheads covered with fabrics, paintings, paneling, and imitation fur, while the deck was carpeted. Some sections were covered with wood and tile. It all added to the total mass of the ship, but Morrison did not worry. He could afford the extra fuel.

"How much longer?" he asked.

Andra glanced at her watch. "Eleven hours."

Morrison shook his head. "We'll miss him. We won't even be close."

"We're at maximum speed," Andra said.

"Damn him. I'm not going to let him get away this time. Raise Walters-Meyer on Lanta 2. Find out what's happening there."

Andra immediately rose and left the lounge. If only they were all like her, he thought. Maybe then I could bear watching them.

I don't even have time to run the business properly anymore. Sherman has hurt me twice over. The mass murders are bad enough on the production schedule, but the time I spend tracking down his chips across the galaxy hurts even more. I've got two hundred planets with mining settlements on them and Sherman has already gotten seven of them. If this keeps up, business is going to really suffer. I can't afford the kind of security organization needed to fight him.

He shifted his weight and the chair creaked. He motioned to the bartender for a fresh drink.

Sherman is on Lanta 2. He couldn't have gotten off the planet yet, Morrison thought. He couldn't have slipped by my men. They're good. That's what I pay them for. He's trapped.

At least I found that meditech who made the chips for Sherman. Too bad that moron killed him.

"Walters-Meyer says they have the network on the alert. That's about as much as he can do right now," Andra said, standing in front of Morrison.

Christ, she's homely, he thought. "All right. Tell the captain to strain the engines—jettison the people if necessary. Then we may not be too late—we may still get him."

3

Donald Sherman enjoyed watching the citizens of Alsis walk past the shops and walkways, going to and from work without the glazed look he had seen on the mining planets. The city had a feel to it, something intangible that spoke of life. It was nothing overt, but the city radiated a feeling of vitality.

He walked along the concrete, watching.

The ride from the spaceport through the underground tube to Alsis had been rapid. He knew that Morrison's men would soon be scouring every city on Lanta 2, but running any farther now was impractical. Boarding a shuttle to another system was more difficult than shorter, intersystem hops. The only remaining planet within the Lanta system which was inhabited, Lanta 3, was a mining planet owned by Morrison. He would have to stay on Lanta 2, locate the underground organization, and stay with them. He needed the safety of hiding for a few months; his subconscious needed time to absorb what he had done. His body needed the rest. There were many deaths before Lanta 1, memories with which he had not yet dealt.

He turned and walked into a store, purchased a local newsfiche, slipped the oily plastic card into his pocket and walked on, eyes always moving, mind always remembering. An apartment was out of the question—moving in and out without baggage would draw unwanted attention, something people would remember.

He would have to make contact with the underground.

The open feeling of the city streets made him edgy. The city plaza was not far off and he decided it would be safer inside. He followed the blue arrows on the walkways until they led him inside the plaza's structure. It cost him valuable time, but he finally located a phonescreen that was smashed and whose camera lens was punctured. He placed two bills in the phonescreen's slot and waited for the muted sound of the dial tone.

An operator came on the line, her monotone informing him the visual circuits were out of order; she suggested he locate another phonescreen. Sherman thanked her and said it would be all right without video. She connected him with Planetary Media Services.

"News, Alsis, classified section, sales," he said.

"One moment," the in-house operator said.

A click, then, "Hello?"

"Yes, hello," Sherman said. "The video is out—I'm calling from a public phonescreen."

"Do you need graphics?" she asked.

"No."

"Good. You can still make the deadline for the next fiche."

Sherman gave her the information he wanted placed in the newsfiche. It was simple and extremely clear to the people he wanted to contact for help.

"That will be seventy-five dollars," the woman said.

Sherman deposited the local currency, almost depleting the change he had received from purchasing the newsfiche. He glanced at his watch. Four hours to wait. Well, no sense being uncomfortable, he thought, looking for a place to relax.

He walked for a few minutes until he came to a grottobar, removed from the mainstream of traffic that flowed by the arcades, stores, theaters, restaurants, sex salons, drug shops, hotels, and other specialty shops that lined the plaza's three levels. A waitress with dark bags under her eyes and a rumpled uniform approached and asked if he wanted a drink.

"Yes," Sherman said. "Make it a Bloody Mary."

"You can go by yourself," Sandy said calmly. She was still in uniform, creases and wrinkles from the long day showing in her clothes and face.

William strode to the kitchen table and sat on a chair, his body angled toward her. "They don't want just me, honey. Don't you see? It's our chance to get away, to be free from all the money-hungry collection agencies."

She laughed softly. "Naive. Jesus, William, don't you realize what you've done?"

"Of course I realize. I've given us a chance for a future. What did we have before?"

"Our freedom, maybe."

"Being in debt, owning nothing, isn't free." William smiled, trying to put Sandy at ease, but the smile felt false, uncomfortable. "Listen, Sandy, they've agreed to pay off all our debts. Every one of them. All we have to do is homestead for them."

She shook her head. "No, William. I won't do it. I'd rather stay here and live like we have been."

"You call this living?" he asked. "I don't. I can't get a job and your salary isn't enough. It's the only way."

"We can live on my salary. We're doing it, aren't we? I know it's not easy, but we can do it. So, they took away most of our furniture—you'll get another job."

"Yeah, right." He pushed himself away from the table and walked down the hallway to the den. He sat on the couch, the only piece of furniture left in the room, and stared blankly at the wall before him.

The holoset used to be there, he thought.

He looked at the mounting brackets for the poles. The repossession company had taken the support poles, all the electronics, but had left him the mounting brackets. William realized he was sitting alone in a dark, empty room, staring at two pieces of metal with holes drilled through them, and feeling depressed.

It wasn't simply that almost everything they had was gone—he could have lived with that. But there was no hope left. Not with Sandy opposed to the help Douglas and the Morrison Mining Company were offering. They had no future. They would have to live day to day, trying to scrape together enough money for rent, food, meditechs, income tax—they would never own anything again.

The room was dark and uncomfortable. Shadows slid past his eyes, through the corners of the room, and he turned to look. It was nothing: just his imagination. He sighed and leaned forward, elbows on his thighs, head cradled in his hands. The room grew darker and he ignored the flickering he saw peripherally.

He couldn't leave Sandy. That was no answer—no solution. Running away would make their debts null and void, but then it would be all over for the two of them as a couple.

He sighed again.

"Do you realize what Douglas wants us to do?"

William looked up at Sandy. He hadn't heard her enter. At first he could only make out her outline; the light from the hallway made the front part of her body blurry, fuzzy.

"Yes, I think I do."

"Tell me then."

"If we don't take this opportunity, we'll probably end up splitting apart. I know that if we go with Douglas, we won't have to. Doesn't that mean anything to you?"

"What are you saying?" she asked, hurt.

William looked back at the mounting brackets. "Jesus. I don't know."

She sat next to him and placed her hand on his shoulder. "What have you heard about this mining company?"

William shrugged.

She leaned back on the couch. "I've been asking around at work and I can't get any facts—just rumors."

"Like?"

30

"Like this whole homesteading setup is not quite as easy as they'd have you believe."

"Who told you this?"

"If it had just been one person, I wouldn't have paid it any mind. One of the men I work with has a brother who was paid a similar visit and signed up with the homesteading operation. He's gotten one communication since his brother left. The brother has become a miner and he and his family have permanently settled on a planet, and they are doing fine."

"A miner? That doesn't sound so bad." William waited for Sandy's reaction, but got none. "At least they were together, free of debts."

"Yes, they were together."

"Doesn't that count?" William asked.

She looked at him and sighed. "Yes, it does. It counts a lot."

At five-thirty, Sherman left the grottobar and walked toward the restaurant. If anyone on Lanta 2 is willing to help, they should be there, waiting, he thought. He walked slowly, like the shoppers, the browsers, the recreationers surrounding him. He did not look at the window displays. He ignored the circuslike entertainment taking place in the central sections and over his head. He did look at every face that passed by.

If even one of those faces held a glimmer of recognition, then he would be discovered. Only Morrison's men knew what he looked like; the surveillance monitors on both the shuttle and in the settlements on Lanta 1 held holograms of his face. Morrison's men would probably already have a copy. Those who were willing to help never knew what he looked like.

It was still early, and the crowds in the plaza were serene, calmly taking in the sights and shops, remembering the locations of those places they would return to later in the evening. Sherman kept a meter between himself and the others. His need to be close and have contact with people was not overwhelming.

He saw a young boy, no more than three or four years old, being dragged along by a woman, who was holding his hand. Probably his mother, Sherman thought. I remember myself at that age— complete confusion, but enjoying the way the confusion dissolved as I grew up and got used to the world. I wasn't much older than that when my parents decided to homestead.

He rubbed the nape of his neck and felt the coolness of metal against his fingers.

I was too young to remember the operation, he thought, and having a slot in the back of my neck didn't bother me then. How old was I, eight? Nine?

And then the first time they inserted a program chip into the receptacle. I'll never forget that feeling. They made me work the mines, too. Half a day at school, half a day in the mines. Still, I did manage to meet Vladimir.

He stopped before the restaurant, checked the jacket pocket for the small, plastic case, and, reassured that the chips were still there, walked inside. The restaurant was not crowded; the bar was empty. He found a stool where his right side would touch a brick wall and sat down. Immediately, the bartender approached.

"What'll it be?"

"Bourbon," Sherman said.

He paid for the drink with a Galactic Draft. The bartender eyed the Draft, then Sherman, then the note again. He looked disgusted.

"This all you got?"

Sherman nodded. "It's good."

"Pain in the ass," the bartender mumbled.

Sherman left the change on the bar and swiveled the stool around so he could see over the low wall separating the bar from the restaurant. It was dark, quiet, the sounds of conversation and silverware striking plates drifted into the bar.

Nice place, Sherman thought.

He glanced at his watch and decided to wait another few minutes.

Within a few minutes of each other, two men came into the bar and sat down, their backs to the restaurant. Sherman looked them over. The first man looked at Sherman, smiled, then ordered a drink. The second man looked familiar.

The light in the bar was dim, and he wished he could make out more of the man's features. As the bartender approached Sherman, he remembered where he had seen the man before. The spaceport. The immigration officer.

The bartender set another drink before Sherman. "From your friend over there. Say's it's to welcome you to our planet," he said.

A chill ran through Sherman.

Two of them? he thought. Maybe there's no decent underground organization on this planet. At least not in Alsis. If the organization had read the ad, they would have sent one man—not two. The balding immigration officer had sat next to the man who had come in right before him.

This stinks, he thought.

Sherman downed the remains of his bourbon. With the immigration officer watching, he raised the fresh glass to his mouth, kept his mouth closed, and tilted the glass back. The balding man walked over.

"Hello again," the man said, offering his hand.

"My name is Philip. Philip Sewel-Tarkington."

Shit. The man didn't even wait for the proper response. "Hello," Sherman said. He grasped the man's hand and felt the chip in his palm.

They sat down.

"Where have you been since this morning?" Philip asked.

"Around." Sherman looked at the other man in the bar and motioned toward him. "Who's he?"

"I thought he might be you. I welcomed him to our planet and he looked at me like I was crazy. He said he was a native." He slipped the chip into his pocket.

Sherman relaxed a little.

"Now, tell me. What happened on Lanta 1?" Philip asked.

"A lot of people died." He tossed off the drink. "I need a place to stay—a place to hide for a while. I have to go underground."

"You can stay with me," Philip offered.

"Oh?"

"We don't have much of an organization in Alsis, or on this planet, for that matter. But then, neither do the mining companies."

"Listen, Philip—I can tell you're a nice guy, and I can see how you're sticking your neck out for me, but I can't stay with you. Understand?"

He watched Philip's eyes and face to see if he did understand. He did not.

"Yes," Philip said.

"I need to be alone for a long time." He motioned for another drink. "I need a place to stay where I'll be safe. I need money, too."

"Okay."

"And if I told you to bite down on one of these?" He held a capsule in his palm.

34

Philip's eyes showed fear. He swallowed with difficulty. "I'd do it."

Sherman did not believe him. He slipped the capsule back into his shirt pocket. The bartender arrived with the drink. Sherman paid for it and told the man to keep the change.

A young couple walked into the bar and sat near the first man who had entered. Sherman glanced out the window to his right. The plaza's activity had picked up in tempo; people walked along, dressed in their finest clothes, wearing the latest fashions of Lanta 2. Sherman wished he could be out there with them, preparing for an evening of festivities.

"Know anyone who wants to be Donald Sherman for a day?"

Philip looked at his half-empty glass, then raised it to his lips. He drained it in one gulp and turned to Sherman who saw the fear in his eyes. The fear went deep—too deep.

"Listen, I'm new to this. If my brother hadn't escaped from Lanta 3, I never would have heard about you. I've got a wife at home. She's good to me, works hard—we take care of each other. My kids are all—"

"Forget it." The dream of walking around safe for a day evaporated. "Forget I even mentioned it."

My luck to get someone like this, he thought. Totally gutless. "Who's that in the restaurant?" When Philip turned to look, he saw the man did not have a receptacle. He felt for the small, plastic case in his jacket, then took a sip of bourbon.

"I don't know. Can we go now?" Philip asked.

"Soon. Have another drink."

"I really shouldn't."

"Bartender," Sherman said, pointing to Philip.

"I don't want another drink."

35

Sherman spun to his left and grabbed Philip's forearm in a tight grip. "Listen, asshole, I didn't ask for you, understand? When I tell you to do something, you do it." He released Philip's arm.

Another young couple came into the bar and sat down several stools away. Sherman sipped his drink. The bartender arrived with Philip's drink, and Sherman paid him.

"What's the age distribution in this city?" Sherman asked Philip.

He shrugged.

"Would you say it's pretty even?" Sherman asked.

"Yeah, I guess so."

Sherman swung around so he could observe the people in the plaza. He leaned forward and touched the large, picture window. It was not glass. He pressed against it, testing its strength.

Another young couple walked in.

"Let's go," Sherman said.

Philip shook his head in confusion, took a last sip, then stood.

"You lead the way."

They walked into the plaza, stopping a few storefronts away. They watched the entrance to the restaurant. Seven people came out. The three couples and the man. Everyone except the bartender. None were smiling. They looked around the plaza anxiously.

Sherman grabbed Philip by the shoulder and pulled him closer to the wall. "Let's go."

4

Benjamin Douglas had made the arrangements quickly. Two days after he had received the phone call, William and Sandy Carter were on their way to the planet Randu to become homesteaders. Douglas had exceeded his recruiting quota for that week and had invested his bonus in Morrison Mining stock. The bonus held a little something extra, since he had persuaded the Carters to homestead on Randu.

"You've got to be kidding," Sandy said.

She stood in the center of the settlement. There were two rows of run-down, wooden structures—

houses. Some of the outside walls were supported by beams of wood wedged between the house and ground. There were no children, no sounds of commotion or activity inside the houses, no signs of life. One man, his face leathery, old, weatherbeaten like the porch he sat on, rocked back and forth slowly, staring into the horizon.

"They must have set us down in the wrong place," William said. "The pilot must have made a mistake."

They put their suitcases down on the dusty, unpaved road and stared at the old man. "It's just like I said it would be," Sandy said.

"It can't be."

"Look," she said, motioning around them with her hands.

"Take it easy, Sandy."

William started walking toward the old man sitting on the porch. "They don't even have electricity," William heard her say to his back. The old man stopped rocking as he approached.

"Hello," William said. "Can you tell us how far it is to the settlement on Randu?"

"You're in it," the man said. "You planning on staying?"

William looked around. "I don't think so." He walked up the creaky porch steps and stood before the man. Up close, William could see his hair was black, graying at the temples. His hands and face were wrinkled, dry and cracked. He looked toughened, tired, beaten; but his eyes did not look old.

"Not many do stay," the man said.

"How long have you been here?" William asked.

"Five years."

William nodded. "That must have been before the age restrictions."

"No," the man said. "I'm forty-two."

38

William looked back at Sandy. "When's the next ship due?"

"Tomorrow. There's one most every day after they set someone down."

Sandy was crying when he reached her side. William held her close and comforted her as best he could.

The pickup ship had arrived just as the settler had predicted. The captain had been all business, explaining to the Carters that they had violated their contract to homestead. He explained that because the Morrison Mining Company had acted in good faith, had absorbed all their debts on Earth, and had provided transportation for them to Randu, they now owed the company a considerable sum. Payable in full. Immediately. He had pointed to the clause in the contract they had signed.

"However," he said, "We are not without understanding."

He gave them a choice of worlds he could set them down on. Every planet was a mining planet.

"In this way," he said, "you can work off your debt."

William and Sandy chose Lanta 3, the last stop the ship would make. They wanted as much time together as possible before becoming miners.

The four months passed too quickly.

The house was nicer than any apartment they had lived in. The food circuits, although archaic like the rest of their appliances, were functional and well stocked. They had room to grow, to raise a family. The house was part of a development, a small section of two hundred homes near the mines.

Everything the Carters bought was expensive, but

after they had worked in the mines for a week, credit became available.

The Morrison Mining Company supplied the house and everything inside it; payment was taken out of their salaries. Transportation costs from Earth to Randu were not mentioned, and William assumed the company had written them off. Transportation from Randu to Lanta 3 was another matter. A size-able chunk of their pay went toward it.

The initial salary had looked good to William and he had been optimistic at first. Sandy knew better.

Situated between the houses and the tram station was a row of shops and buildings. The Carters could buy anything they wanted. Until their credit ran out.

It was morning, and William was asleep. Sandy sat up in bed carefully, not wanting to wake him. The night before he had been out alone, and stayed out late.

She propped herself up with her pillow and leaned back, the metal slot in her neck pressing against the cool pillowcase.

It was a small price to pay, the meditech had told her after they put the receptacle in. She did not agree.

It was 5:00—still time to catch another fifteen minutes, she thought. She readjusted her pillow and tried to sleep. She rolled onto her side, trying to get comfortable, and felt the coolness of the air on the nape of her neck. A chill ran down her back.

She snuggled closer to William.

Sherman walked slowly, knowing that seven agents were following them. The bourbon felt good, warmth spreading from his stomach through his body.

"Let's stop in here," Sherman said, pointing to a shop a few meters ahead.

"All right," Philip said. "Can I call my wife first?"

Sherman grabbed him by the elbow and stopped. He swung Philip around to face him.

"What's my name?"

"Donald Sherman."

"Tell your wife you are entertaining me. She'll understand."

They walked into the drug shop.

The interior of the shop was ornate, designed for hours of mindless browsing. Small alcoves were set into the walls; most of them were occupied. The walls themselves changed color constantly. To the rear of the shop was a woman, eyes glassy, face muscles slack, sitting on a stool behind a counter.

"I don't respond well to hallucinogens," Philip said.

"Don't worry. Give me all your money."

Philip hesitated a moment, then reached into his pocket. He withdrew several hundred dollar bills and some smaller bills. He gave it all to Sherman.

"The organization will reimburse you."

"I hope so," Philip said.

Sherman slowly shook his head. He approached the counter.

"May I help you." The woman spoke slowly, flatly.

"Yes. I'm having a party tonight and I wondered what you had in the way of misting canisters."

"For how many people."

"Oh, twelve couples."

"Let me see what we have left."

Sherman smiled and watched her go into the back room. He turned and looked toward the front of the shop; two of the couples were already inside, walking through the displays. He could see another couple standing by the door.

Too smart to all come in at once, Sherman thought. The couples were getting closer.

"Do you know any of them?" Sherman asked Philip.

"No."

"Can you pretend you do?"

"I—I don't know."

"How about if your life depended on it?"

Philip nodded.

"Go over to them. Be loud. Slap them on the back. Ask why you haven't seen them around. Be very friendly, Sewel-Tarkington, understand?"

Philip nodded and walked away. The woman returned with a misting canister.

"How long does it take for the drug to work?"

"Seconds we've never had a complaint," she said.

"Uhm, how does this model activate?"

"Just place it on a table or the floor in the middle of the room and press this button."

He didn't know if the shop had a back door. He didn't know if *any* of the stores in the plaza had back doors. "Just put it down and press this?" Sherman asked.

Philip had the two couples occupied, but they were nervous, and too quiet. Sherman thought that Philip was strained to his maximum and would break momentarily.

"Yes just press that will this be cash or charge?" she asked.

"Charge," Sherman said.

He placed the canister by his feet and reached into his pocket. He withdrew his identification card and dropped it. He reached down to pick it up with his left hand. He pressed the start button on the misting canister with his right.

One lungful of fresh air, he thought as he kicked the metal tube toward the couples and Philip Sewel-Tarkington. The tube bounced, then rolled about two meters. Then the fogger came on. It filled the shop with a fine mist of hallucinogens.

He leaped over the counter and ran by the woman. She was about to yell something, but as she inhaled, she took in a lungful of the penetrating mist.

Sherman ran into the stockroom and slammed the door shut. He ran up and down the aisles, trying to find the exit. He saw an opening, an aisle to his right, and walked through it.

The door was directly before him. He grabbed the knob and turned it, took a few ragged breaths and pushed open the exit door. He tried to calm his heart and get his breathing under control. He fell into the alley, choking, gasping for breath.

The ship-to-ground shuttle brought Morrison and Andra to Lanta 2. When the shuttle's sterilization procedures were over, the door in the side of the craft slid open. A man was waiting at the bottom of the ladder. Beside him stood two more men.

Morrison made his way down the steps awkwardly. He could not see the steps before him. A man at the bottom approached, extended his hand. "Mr. Morrison? I'm Walters-Meyer."

He was taller than Morrison, and Morrison stopped his descent before his feet were touching the concrete. On the last step he was a few centimeters taller than Walters-Meyer. He ignored the outstretched hand. "If you're Walters-Meyer, then Donald Sherman had better not be on this planet."

"He's here. My men have him under surveillance."

Morrison was shocked. "Then what are you doing here? Why aren't you watching him, too?"

"My man has him under control. One of my best

agents, Sewel-Tarkington, is with Sherman right now."

Morrison raised his eyebrows.

"Sherman thinks my man is his contact."

"Good, good." He finished his descent. Andra followed him down the ladder. He waited for her.

"It sounds like you're doing a good job," Andra said.

"I'm trying to. He wasn't that difficult to find after all."

"Sherman? Easy to find? We must not be talking about the same person." Morrison shook his head and scowled. "There's something wrong, Andra. Get back on board and radio the ship. Have them send down some men as soon as possible."

"My men can handle this," Walters-Meyer said. He looked confident and a little insulted.

"Fine, but just in case they don't, I'd like to make sure Sherman doesn't get away. If he gets off this planet, I'll do to you what I plan to do to him." He turned back to Andra. "Have the men set up a security search of all the spaceports on this planet until it's over. Do we know what he looks like this time?" he asked Walters-Meyer.

"Yes." He reached into his coat and withdrew a low quality hologram.

"That's one hell of an ugly person," Morrison said. Andra said nothing.

"Well? Where is he?" Morrison demanded.

"A few hundred kilometers away. I suggest we leave now."

Morrison shook his head in disgust. "Those bastards wouldn't give us clearance for any 'port closer." He turned to Andra. "We'll wait for you. Send that message now."

She climbed aboard Morrison's shuttle. Morrison watched Walters-Meyer. He seems calm enough, he thought. Not intimidated by my presence at all. Perhaps he can be of some use in the future.

"How much do I pay you?" Morrison asked.

"Four hundred thousand."

He nodded. A decent salary, enough to live on in relative comfort. About what a cheaper house would cost on a lesser colony.

"You married?"

"No." Walters-Meyer stopped slouching and straightened his shoulders. He was unused to the attention.

Morrison watched the man fidget. He knew he couldn't stand up to close scrutiny. They're all the same, Morrison thought. Andra returned from the shuttle and stood by his side. "All right then, Walters-Meyer. It's time we moved in for the kill," Morrison said.

He thought he saw Walters-Meyer grimace, but he couldn't be sure.

They climbed into the aircar.

The afternoon on Lanta 3 was cold. It was midsummer, and the red dwarf Lanta warmed the planet to a barely comfortable temperature. The Carters had eaten their lunches together and were back in the mines, chips reinserted, working.

That morning, they had received new chips and had been ordered to a new section.

William manned a monitoring machine inside the checking station. It was his responsibility to scan the cross-section of molten metal for fluid dynamic stress points. The metal was kept under constant high pressure.

The lowest level of metal was red. This ran up for ten meters and then shifted in hue to orange. This strata was more volatile and demanded more careful monitoring. Seven meters above the orange came a strata of blue. William skimmed up and down his length of glassite-enclosed metal constantly watching, constantly checking. He rode the air platform like he had ridden it all his life. He watched with the knowledge of a specialized technician with decades of training and experience.

William enjoyed one thing about having the chip: while he worked, he could detach his personality. He had to do nothing to control his body's movements, and this allowed him time to relax, think, or even let his conscious mind sleep.

Although the feeling was unique, there were aspects that were unpleasant. There were times when a simple thing like an itch would drive him crazy. He would try to scratch it, but the program chip would need his hands elsewhere. There were times when he saw Sandy but could not say hello. He was aware inside his own body and yet had no control over it.

He found that if he let his concentration drift he could sleep. Once he woke up a few hours after lunch to find himself falling. The chip had been removed while he slept and his conscious mind had not taken back control of his body in time.

Working for the Morrison Mining Company isn't as bad as some people make it out to be, he thought. But then there are troublemakers wherever you go, giving you the answers to questions you never asked. The way they talk you'd think they weren't cared for.

William's shift ended and after turning in the workchip, he set out to meet Sandy. He found her waiting by the tram. They embraced and kissed. They boarded the train and it sped back to town, letting them off in the shopping area.

"Don't even look," Sandy warned as they headed for home.

"I wasn't going to," William lied.

He thought about how their lives had changed since they had met Douglas. He could see one major difference: he and Sandy were, and would remain, together. If they wanted or needed something, all they had to do was buy it. Their salaries were attached but their credit was still good.

Sandy was quiet and seemed upset about something. They usually talked on their walk home, exchanging stories about what kind of work they had done during the day.

"What's the matter?" he asked.

"Nothing."

"Come on. I know you better than that. What's bothering you? Did I say something?"

"No, William, it's not you." She sighed. "I might as well tell you—I'm nervous about tonight."

"What, that meeting?"

"Yes."

They walked along in silence for a few moments, then Sandy looked up at her husband. "William?"

"Yes?"

"What do you think they want to talk to us about?"

"I don't know. Probably something about production schedules being off. I don't think it's anything to worry about."

Sandy still looked upset.

"What are you worrying about it for? It's not like it's a surprise or anything—it's on the company calendar."

She nodded. "Yeah, I guess so."

The evening air was chilling.

"I wouldn't have minded if you'd killed him," Morrison said.

"I didn't think you would. I just thought you might

47

like to take him alive. For questioning," Walters-Meyer said.

The two men sat in the aircar's back seat. There was no room for Andra, so she sat in front with Walters-Meyer's two men.

"I would like to talk to him. I would like to talk to him very much. But not at the risk of letting him get away." Morrison folded his hands across his stomach.

Helene wants to talk to him, too, Morrison thought. I don't want them to meet—it could turn into something potentially dangerous. I can't even trust her anymore. A few months ago I would have never taken her along on this trip. Bobbi, yes. Andra, of course. But Helene? My God. But I couldn't have left her on Earth—not with my main offices there.

"We can't do anything overt while he's in public places," Walters-Meyer said. "If we do, we'll have the local police to contend with."

Morrison nodded.

"We'll be over Alsis in about five minutes," one of the men in the front said.

"Good. My men should have everything under control. Eight people are more than enough to take care of anyone."

"Almost anyone," Morrison said. "I don't think you fully realize whom you're dealing with."

"I know all about him. To me, he's a murderer. That's all."

"That may be, but he's got a cause. He doesn't want to kill."

"Right," Walters-Meyer said.

At least that's what Helene keeps telling me, Morrison thought. Sherman doesn't want to kill. She says he's psychotic. It's difficult for me to accept—more difficult than it is for Walters-Meyer. At least he knows or seems to know what he's doing. But then, that's why I hired him.

It would be so much simpler if Sherman bothered someone else. There are plenty of other mining companies. He must be obsessed. And that goddamn Interplanetary Monitor Agency is no help at all. They don't qualify as a police force. I'm probably supporting half the agency just by my payoffs. What the hell good are they? Monitors. Shit. They keep an eye on all the interplanetary trade for those who belong and impose fines when an agreement is broken. And the independents don't even belong.

Maybe Sherman will go for a deal. Maybe I can buy that bastard off. Christ, I wish I knew.

"Here we are," Walters-Meyer said.

"Good."

They all got out of the aircar and waited for Morrison to make his slow and cumbersome exit. He was having trouble getting enough leverage to pull himself out of the tilted seat until one of Walters-Meyer's men gave him a hand. Morrison did not thank him.

Morrison looked at the tremendous building before him. He hadn't expected seeing such a large, well-designed, striking building in Alsis. He had always thought of Lanta 2 as a second-rate Independent. "What the hell is this place?"

"The city's main plaza," Walters-Meyer said.

"Interesting. Primitive, but interesting."

Walters-Meyer led them through the nearest entrance into the enclosed plaza. As they entered, Morrison admired the interior design. There were two levels of shops directly before him; down toward his left they split into three levels, then back to two, with openings and passageways between the shops.

Walters-Meyer had removed a small communicator from his pocket and was speaking into it. He listened to the tinny voice and then held it up so Morrison could see the dots of light indicating the speaker's relative distance and location. His face was drained of blood as he slipped the disk back into his pocket.

"What is it?" Morrison demanded.

"He escaped."

Morrison tightened his lips and turned to Andra. "How long before the men from our ship land?"

"Not soon enough to cover all the exits," she said. "I doubt if they're set up in all the spaceports yet."

He wheeled back to Walters-Meyer. "Well? This is your fiasco—what do you suggest?" Morrison asked, realizing that nothing could be done.

"Let's go to where he was last seen—maybe we can learn something there. I want to talk to my men."

Morrison shook his head, trying to control his rage.

They walked through the passageways, went up and down escalators until they stood before a small drug shop. Morrison had to push aside a man with long, blond hair and drooping eyelids so he could see what happened. The front window of the store was shattered, and Philip Sewel-Tarkington lay face down in a pool of blood and glass. Four of Walters-Meyer's men sat on the carpeting holding their heads, looking drained and disoriented. The rest of his people milled through the rapidly growing crowd, searching.

Walters-Meyer approached Sewel-Tarkington's body.

Two local policemen questioned witnesses and Andra got close to one, listened to the flow of conversation for a few minutes, then handed the officer

50

a business card. The policeman answered her questions, explaining what had happened. When he finished, she walked back to Morrison.

"As near as they can figure it, Sewel-Tarkington went through the window by his own force," she said.

"Suicide?" Walters-Meyer asked. "Not him."

"Leave it," Morrison told him. "Continue."

"Apparently, a man walked into the shop to buy a misting canister for a party he was having and it went off accidentally. The drug had a bad effect on Sewel-Tarkington's nervous system—or his stability," Andra said.

Morrison's stomach tightened. "He's gone."

5

Sherman was nineteen years old when his parents died. He watched Morrison's men dig up the earth of Sanbar 5 with anger and hatred blazing in his eyes. The sun had almost set and friends of the Shermans stood by and watched in silence.

The people of the mining settlement had always liked the Shermans. They had been neighborly, helpful when others were in need. Now, they were dead.

A young Sherman pushed his jet-black hair behind his ears and tried to look stoic. The hair fell over the nape of his neck to his shoulders, covering the slot. A man who had been a minister on a planet far away from Sanbar 5 intoned words to which Sherman paid no attention. Insects came out in the cool twilight and their noises blended with the ex-minister's voice.

"I'm very sorry, Donald," Vladimir Leaw-Zabinski said.

Sherman looked up at the tall, lanky man on his left. Vladimir was staring at the ground by his feet. Donald noticed how much older Vladimir looked.

Vladimir was a top-rated meditech—a man who had taken part in designing the receptacles for the chips. It was his idea to place them farther down the nervous system, farther away from the medulla oblongata. Donald's fascination with the chip and receptacle system had led to a friendship with Vladimir.

"That's all right, Vladimir. I know you're not responsible for this."

"You can't change what I feel," Vladimir said softly.

When the last shovel of sandy earth had been thrown onto the graves, people walked over to Donald to pay their respects.

"Buy little, save, and prosper," they said.

Donald nodded and thanked each of them, remembering when they and his parents had played cards, or gone camping, or just talked for hours. For each person there was a different warm memory. He recalled little incidents and stories his parents had talked about and he shared these with their friends. When all the people had left, Donald stood alone under a starlit sky, staring at the two fresh graves.

He thought of the Morrison Mining Company and how it had murdered his parents. Conversations he and Vladimir had came back to him clearly.

"No other company uses the same method, Donald."

"Why not?"

Vladimir hadn't told him. The information had come years later, when Donald was studying biology in school.

"What do the other mining companies do, then?"

"Some companies teach their people how to perform one job. It takes years to learn how to operate some of the equipment, and some people aren't capable of understanding what it is they actually do."

"The company selects those with lower capabilities," Donald said.

"No, not really. You can't expect anyone to fully grasp something that is so complex. It can take years to learn where to put your hands without ever understanding why you're putting them there."

Standing before the graves, he remembered other stories Vladimir had told him. There were companies that used RNA injections to give their workers the equivalent of years of experience and instant understanding. Donald had remarked of the similarity between the chip and receptacle system, and the RNA system.

"There are similarities, but the differences are what caused Morrison to choose this system. The RNA permanently changes the injected person. It's also harder on production. If someone becomes ill, there's no way for him to be replaced just for the day. Sometimes all production stops when one metal worker is out. Then, there are cost factors, too."

Donald had smiled.

It wasn't until years later that he began questioning Vladimir about his personal life. Vladimir was Donald's adopted uncle, a relationship they both easily slipped into. The more time Vladimir and Donald spent together, the less Donald could understand what he was doing on a planet like Sanbar 5.

"I made a mistake once," Vladimir had said.

"But still, you don't deserve to live here. You help develop the system for him, and then he throws you out, sends you to this planet."

"It was a big mistake."

"What did you do?"

Vladimir looked into Donald's eyes. "I was married once. We were both young when I went to work for Morrison. I had known him during a war. It was a little different before—well, after my associates and I had a disagreement over the physical placement of the receptacle, things started changing. At first I didn't think anything of it. Morrison was friendly to us both, but I later found out he was more friendly toward my wife."

"What did you do?"

"I made a mistake by accusing him of the truth." Vladimir paused before continuing. "He already had my wife so he didn't harm me. He just sent me here."

Donald watched the man's face as he talked. He could see the hurt and pain and did not want to push him any further.

"I received notification of our divorce, though it wasn't necessary," Vladimir said.

The chill of the evening crept through Donald's shirt. The smell of freshly turned earth was in his nose, and the night insects' buzzing filled his ears. All the friends had left the cemetery. The mourners would try to forget what had happened to the Shermans, be thankful it had not happened to them, and hope they would not be next.

Donald knew who was responsible for his parents' death. And his parents were not the only ones to die like this; it was murder.

55

"Donald?"

He was startled and wheeled around. "Oh, it's you, Vladimir."

"Have you decided what you're going to do yet?"

"No."

"Standing here isn't going to change anything," Vladimir said. "Two of the company's representatives are waiting for you at your house."

My house, he thought. "What do they want?"

Vladimir shrugged. "Who knows?" Donald did not move. "I'll go along with you. Come on."

"Thank you, Vladimir."

Vladimir smiled and put a protective arm around the young man's shoulders. "You're welcome."

The house was dark except for the living room. The overhead lighting panel was on; brilliance spilled out the windows illuminating the native flowers in the front garden. Donald could see two men through the window. He glanced up at his friend, pushed his hair behind his ears, and strode up the front porch steps.

He pushed open the screen door and stood in the foyer, arms crossed tightly, waiting for one of them to say something.

One of the men looked about ten or fifteen pounds overweight, had wild red hair and a scraggly beard starting red at his sideburns, gradually turning blond. The other was thin, wore wire-rimmed glasses, and sported a neatly trimmed Van Dyke. The heavy one rose and approached Donald, hand extended. Donald saw only the man's eyes. The man stopped a pace away.

"Donald Sherman?"

Donald made no reply. Vladimir stood in front of the door, watching, listening. The red-head lowered his hand and Donald saw his eyes harden.

56

"My name is Kingsley-Arcadia. I'm sorry about your parents' deaths."

Sherman did not move.

"I said—"

"I heard what you said. What do you want?" Donald demanded.

"Why, you pompous little bastard. Just who do you think you are?"

"Easy, Kings," his companion said, rising from the easy chair and striding over to him. "You must forgive my friend's short temper, Mr. Sherman. I always have to jump in and calm him down. You see, he doesn't understand the way you feel."

Vladimir smiled wryly. Donald's expression did not change. His face showed no feeling.

"Kingsley doesn't get along too well with people, Mr. Sherman. I keep telling him that if he doesn't change his ways, he's going to get himself into big trouble. Right, Kings?"

"Right," the red-headed man monotoned.

"And even so, it doesn't seem to do much good. He still loses his temper, still causes trouble." He shook his thin head thoughtfully. "My name is Neubaur-Butler. Mr. Kingsley-Arcadia and I are here to help you straighten out your parents' estate." He motioned with his hand, inviting Donald into the living room.

Donald was torn. The man was polite and understanding, but he was still one of Morrison's men. If he relaxed and let down his guard, he would be put in a defensive position. Neubaur-Butler was disarming, but that's like Morrison, Sherman realized, to send two men; if strong-arm fails, there's always charm.

"Don't you want to straighten out the estate now? We could wait a few days, if you'd rather."

"No. We'll do it now."

He waited for Morrison's men to reseat themselves. When Kingsley-Arcadia had his back to him, Donald noticed the slot in the back of the man's neck. He was surprised at first, but he realized that at one time, the man must have been a miner. He must have done something—uncovered some sabotage, turned someone in, given the support some higher-up needed at the right time. There were ways to get out of the mines.

Donald and Vladimir sat across from Morrison's representatives. Neubaur-Butler absently stroked his Van Dyke while staring into an open briefcase on the table before him. The house was silent for several moments and, despite the discomfort, Donald was resolved not to say or do anything to help them. Vladimir cleared his throat and Morrison's men looked up.

"Well, Mr. Sherman, I see your house isn't completely paid for as of yet, but we are willing to let you remain here if you continue with the same payment schedule as your parents had," Neubaur-Butler said. "We can deduct your payment from your salary at the mine."

"What salary?" Donald asked. "What makes you think I'm going back to the mines?"

Kingsley-Arcadia laughed. "That's a good one, it is."

"Shut up, Kings. Not going back to the mines?" Neubaur-Butler asked. "Why wouldn't you want to go back?"

"I don't want to work there anymore."

"Well, I can understand that. You feel the mines were responsible for your parents' deaths. I'm sure you don't want to believe me now, but your parents died of natural causes."

"You don't understand," Donald said. "I don't think working in the mines had anything to do with their deaths. I'm just not going to work in the mines anymore."

"And what will you do for food? Shelter?"

"That's my problem."

"Indeed it is," Kingsley-Arcadia said.

Neubaur-Butler glanced at his fellow representative, then turned back to Sherman. "I take it, then, that you're asking for a different job?"

"No, I'm not."

Neubaur-Butler smiled. "Well now, Mr. Sherman, I can see the strain of today's unfortunate experience has been too much for you." He turned to Vladimir. "Perhaps you could talk some sense to the boy."

"Donald is not a boy, and if I did talk sense to him, it would be my sense—not his. Other people's reasoning is quickly discarded when it doesn't agree with your own," Vladimir said.

"Do you realize that if you don't work the mines you can't stay in this house?"

"Yes."

"Sanbar 5 is a big planet, Sherman, and this isn't the only mining settlement. Perhaps a transfer a few hundred kilometers away . . ."

Sherman said nothing.

"Very well, then. The receptacle and reading mechanisms implanted in your body are yours. Take whatever clothes you want." He turned to his associate. "Close the house after he leaves, Kingsley, then meet me at the office."

"At this hour?" Kingsley-Arcadia asked.

"Yes. At this very hour."

Donald went into the room he had lived in for the past ten years and gathered up the bundle he had prepared that morning. Alone in his bedroom, isolated, he felt his parents' presence strongly. He could almost hear his parents' voices filtering through the wall that separated their bedrooms, talking over the day's events. He smiled and returned to the living room. Neubaur-Butler had left, but Vladimir and Kingsley-Arcadia remained, waiting for him.

Sleep had not come for Donald. The night had passed slowly. The stainless steel examining table was uncomfortable despite its padded cushions. He felt weak, drained; his eyes burned and his stomach growled. He heard the click of the clinic's door being unlocked and jumped to his feet.

It was Vladimir.

Donald sat back on the edge of the table. "Good morning."

Vladimir smiled. "Good morning. I was afraid you wouldn't still be here."

"I told you I'd stay. Did they bother you last night?"

"No." Vladimir closed the door and entered the room. He walked around quietly, opening all the doors and peering into the rooms. "Anyone bother you here?"

"No. It was quiet."

Vladimir completed his checking, then pressed the button on the coffee dispenser. "I don't know if that's good or bad."

Donald did not smile.

"What are your plans? You can't stay here for long. The reps will be back, you know. If you stay with me at my house they'll charge you rent. I don't own it outright yet."

"I understand, Vladimir. I'm going to get off Sanbar 5. I'm going to destroy Alexander Franklin Morrison."

He handed Donald a cup of coffee. "You're what?"

"You heard me. I'm going to get Morrison." He tasted the coffee. It was bitter, but warming.

"You're serious?"

"I am."

"Then you're as good as dead."

"And if I stayed on this planet? What would I be?"

Vladimir frowned and sipped his coffee. "I admire your goal, Donald, but getting to Morrison—it just can't be done. He lives on Earth; exactly where on Earth, no one seems to know. All of his buildings have incredibly tight security systems. If you were to walk into one carrying a weapon, you wouldn't get two meters inside before his men were all over you. It would be suicide."

"He murdered my parents and hundreds of other miners. He's totally without regard for other human beings—he neither knows nor cares about our suffering. I have no future here." He finished the coffee in the cup. "I have no future anywhere. Why shouldn't I try?"

Vladimir nodded. "Indeed. Why not?"

Donald was groggy. He tried to sit up but he was too weak. He could not remember where he was or what was happening to him. His thoughts were slow, muddy; when he tried to pin down any one thought, it slid away. He tried to talk, to ask someone where he was, what was happening, but no sounds emerged. He struggled against the floating feeling, tried to grab onto a name, an idea, anything.

The image of a man formed in his mind. The benevolent smile on the man's face did not seem to fit. As Donald lost consciousness, one thought came through clearly: destroy that man.

"Donald?"

He opened his eyes and saw Vladimir.

"You're coming out of the anesthetic now. How do you feel?"

"A little disoriented. What happened?"

"You don't remember?"

He concentrated for a moment. "The chips. You were going to make the chips. Did it work?"

"I don't know yet. We'll have to wait until you feel better before we test them. I'll have to call someone . . ."

Donald started to sit up but felt too weak. Two strong hands grabbed him by the shoulders and helped him. The room rocked back and forth a moment, then steadied. He pushed his shoulder blades back and helped support himself by grasping the edge of the table.

"Feel like you can walk around?" Vladimir asked.

"No, not yet."

"Take your time."

Donald remained on the edge of the table until his nausea passed. He walked around the room unsteadily, holding onto chairs and countertops when necessary. When he had made a full circuit he stopped before Vladimir.

"How long was I out?"

"The better part of the day. The sun's down already."

"The equipment—do you think it worked?"

"The modifications could have been done by any Class-A meditech who wanted to spend the time and effort figuring it out. But I never met a meditech who would have thought of trying it. Even if one had, he

62

never would have taken the chance. If he was caught..."

The chips were sitting in a small, foam-lined, plastic shipping case.

"What's the red one for?" Donald asked.

"It's your mind, like the white chips, but it lacks any motor control. If you were to insert this chip, you wouldn't be able to control any of the person's actions, but you would know what they were thinking. Not to any great depths, mind you, just the upper personality levels. The person you would be inside would know all about you, your experiences, your life."

"Why? It sounds worthless," Donald said.

"I've done this for you—now do something for me. Grant me my one dream. I know Morrison has a receptacle; I implanted it myself. If you do get to him, slip the red chip in. I don't expect it to happen, Donald. I expect you to die quite soon."

"So do I. Let's just hope it's not too soon."

Vladimir called a friend and invited him over to the clinic. He asked him not to say anything to anyone about the visit. The man came willingly.

When his friend walked through the doorway, he looked upset.

"Donald, you know Carson, don't you?" Vladimir asked from behind his desk.

"Yes." Donald nodded to the man. "How are you, Carson?"

"Fine. I'm sorry to hear about your parents. I liked them."

"Good," Vladimir said, rising. "That's one of the reasons why I asked you to come here and not someone else."

Carson looked confused.

"I trust you with my life, Carson."

"What's this all about?"

"I'm afraid I can't tell you that."

"It's serious then?"

"Yes."

Carson sat down across from Donald. Donald could see the man searching his face for an answer, probing his eyes. He remained firm, expressionless.

"We need your help," Vladimir said.

"What kind of help?"

"I'm going to anesthetize you for an hour or so. At the end of the hour you can go home."

"No explanations?"

"None."

"I'll give you one," Donald said. "It may help us all get rid of Alexander Franklin Morrison."

"I'll do it."

The anesthetic took five seconds to take effect and lasted one minute. After Carson was unconscious, Vladimir asked Donald to go into an adjoining room and not come out until he called him. He warned that no matter what he heard, he was to stay inside the other room. Donald left and Vladimir inserted the first white chip in the back of Carson's neck.

He opened his eyes slowly, head groggy.

"How do you feel?"

"Disoriented," Carson said. "What happened?"

Vladimir frowned. "Concentrate."

He concentrated for a moment. "The chips. Did you make them? Do they work?"

A smile spread across Vladimir's face—the first real smile in years. He explained to Donald that he was in Carson's body. He saw the shock register on Carson's face. Vladimir calmed him down by talking to him, soothing him, explaining that the original Donald Sherman was in the next room. When Donald understood and had accepted that he was a chip, he got up and walked awkwardly around the room, trying out Carson's body.

"It feels different. It's not the same at all."

"No, I didn't think it would be," Vladimir said.

After a few minutes, he had Donald sit down again.

"Listen, Donald. I'm going to have to repeat this procedure three more times for the other white chips. All the other chips have to know what I've told you and they have to be tested, too. If you are the one inserted, you will become instantly aware, instantly conscious. But you may not know where you are or what is expected of you. Do you understand?"

Donald nodded.

"You'll have to test that red chip some time in the future. Don't worry about that now. If you work, then it should." He injected the sedative into Carson's body.

He repeated the procedure while Donald kept his ear pressed to the door in the other room, fascinated and horrified.

"They work better than I thought they would," Vladimir said. "They seem to block out the person's conscious mind entirely."

"No memories, then," Donald said.

"Yes. No memories for them."

Donald held the small, plastic case in his hand. "Well, Vladimir, thank you."

"Don't thank me, Donald. Just succeed."

He left Vladimir and set off for the spaceport. Kingsley-Arcadia was scheduled to board the off planet shuttle. Donald planned to be on it.

6

"Are you going to get ready?" William asked, placing the plastic trays into the foodwall for re-cycling.

Sandy nodded.

The foodwall hummed and clicked as it processed the trays. Its antique circuits and mechanisms needed servicing, but Sandy had insisted that it could wait.

She looked tired. Her fatigue was more than physical; even when they had been on Earth, with her working longer, harder hours, she had never looked this bad, William realized.

Her face was expressionless, her eyes empty.

William reluctantly left her sitting at the kitchen table and went up to the bedroom to dress. He selected an orange thermalsuit from his closet and laid it on the bed. He undressed and threw his wadded-up clothing into the chute in the wall to be cleaned, folded, and stored. The reassuring click of the apparatus did not come.

He was annoyed and, pressing the chute inward, saw his clothes heaped at the bottom of the slide. He swore silently. First the foodwall, now this, he thought. As if the repair bill wasn't going to be large enough with just one breakdown.

Sighing, he went into the bathroom to clean up. He did not hurry himself; there was not much time, but he did not want to rush back into the bedroom only to find Sandy not ready. He would give her as much time as possible.

But when he walked out of the bathroom, Sandy was sitting on the edge of the bed, still not ready.

"What's the matter? Are you all right?"

"Yes, fine."

She didn't sound fine, but there was no time to press her. It was probably something he had said or done hours, or even days, earlier. She had a habit of holding inside whatever was bothering her until, days later, blown far out of proportion, she would explode.

"Are you going to get dressed?"

She sat there, staring at the floor.

"Sandy? Are you going to get ready? We're going to be late." He tried to keep his voice even.

She looked up at him. "Go without me."

"Funny."

"I mean it. Go without me. I don't want to go."

"We have to go. Both of us."

She shook her head. "No. Not me. Not this time. I

68

don't like it here, I don't like this house the people the guards the cameras the mines—"

"I think I get the point," he said sharply. "Look, I don't like them either." His voice softened. "But we're here and we have to make the best of the situation."

"Oh?"

"That's right."

"Why?"

It was developing into something for which they had no time. Maybe after the meeting. "We'll talk about this later. Right now, get ready to go."

"I've already told you I'm not going."

"Sandy."

"I don't see any sense in going to a meeting."

"It's not the meeting, then, is it?"

"What do you mean?"

"You don't care one way or another about this meeting, do you?"

She shrugged.

"All right," he said, sighing. "I don't like it here, either. You want to get out of here."

She smiled sardonically. "Shall I pack now?"

He shook his head. "No. Just get ready for the meeting. We'll talk about getting off this planet later, when we get home."

She did not move. William crossed the room and sat beside her on the edge of the bed. He held her hands and she turned to face him.

"Baby, this is important. If we don't show up for this meeting we could be in big trouble, and then we'd never get out of here. They'd be watching us all the time."

"They're already watching," she said.

"You know what I mean—they're watching, I know, but they're not looking for anything."

"And how do you plan to get us out of here? There are all of two spaceports on Lanta 3."

"I don't know yet. Give me some time to work on it."

"Sure. We've got plenty of time."

"Will you go to the meeting now?"

She nodded grudgingly.

William put on his orange thermalsuit. He stepped onto the platform in his closet and a pair of thermalboots were sprayed over his stockinged feet. They dried in seconds. He looked at himself in the full-length mirror and smiled. Still in his prime.

Christ, he thought. I don't want to leave. What the hell did I agree to that for? So we're in debt. So what? What is she making such a big thing out of it for? We've been in debt before—she should be used to it by now. We've never had it so good.

All right—the house is a little old-fashioned and the conveniences aren't the latest, but it's not primitive. All we owe is to the company, and they're not about to throw me or Sandy out of work—not until we pay them back, at least.

The jobs aren't bad, either. The chips make them easy to do; all you have to do is show up. So it'll take us some time to pay what we owe, but we'll do it. She'll probably calm down and realize how good our situation is once she thinks about it.

"Ready."

William turned away from the mirror and looked at his wife. She wore more makeup than usual and it helped cover the lifelessness on her face. "You look good," he said.

"Let's go," she said.

Sherman could not get enough air.

He was choking, gasping for breath, then lapsing into spells of panting. The alley was cool and he felt the air currents created by the air-conditioning system flow over his face and hands.

He pushed himself up onto his knees and rested for a few moments. His mind was functioning normally; but he realized his thoughts were too clear, too unmuddled for his reaction to have come from the hallucinogenic drug.

Even in an allergenic reaction, there would have to have been sufficient quantities of the drug in his system to affect his thought process, too. Unless, of course, he was not really suffocating. He quickly ruled that out.

He had to get out of the alley and back into the plaza. The valuable time he had gained by incapacitating Morrison's men in the drug shop was quickly slipping away. They would come after him as soon as they were able.

Sherman pushed himself off his knees and stood shakily. Dizzy, he leaned against the wall for support, constantly trying to maintain control of the body he was occupying. He leaned forward, and this shift in weight started him off down the alley.

The sprayed concrete walls were rough and tore into his right side as he stumbled away from the shop. His breathing became less regulated.

This is what it must have been like for my parents, he thought. Knowing, lying in bed, waiting for your body to die while there's nothing you can do about it, mind fully aware, thinking clearly while the medulla's functions slowly disintegrate.

He tried to remember how long he had been in the scarred man's body. Months, he knew. Well before Lanta 1. Each time he remembered a planet he had been on, a village or town destroyed, his mind drifted back to the problem of breathing.

The alley was poorly lit; the dull glow from the overhead lighting panels was barely enough to keep from tripping, falling. As he walked, he checked each door he passed, but each was locked. He tried forcing one and the more pressure he applied, the dizzier he became. Sherman gave it up and continued walking.

More important than finding an exit was finding a new body. Someone implanted with a receptacle on Lanta 2, willingly or not, would have to give his body.

The first time he had taken someone else's body without Vladimir's help had been a frightening experience. Everything had been different; his sensory perceptions had been out of balance from what he was used to. He had learned to adjust after the week spent in Kingsley-Arcadia's body while escaping from Sanbar 5.

He wondered how many brain cells were already killed by oxygen starvation.

A door slid open and the light that glared through momentarily blinded him. He shielded his eyes with his hand and heard the door slide shut. Someone grabbed his shoulders and pushed him to the floor. He blinked rapidly and his eyes became adjusted to the dim lighting again.

"Sherman?"

The man had long, blond hair and drooping eyelids. He unclenched his fist. Resting in his palm was a chip.

Sherman tried to speak, but could not. He nodded his head in answer.

"You're in bad shape. Come on. Let's get you out of here."

Sherman shook his head. He reached into his jacket pocket and pulled out the small, plastic case. He withdrew a white chip from its recess, made a circular motion with his finger, and the man turned around, grabbing his hair and pulling it aside to expose a slot. "I have to talk with you," the man said. "I have to explain—it wasn't my—"

Sherman inserted the chip.

The stores were not open that evening. As they walked toward the meeting hall, William and Sandy recognized many people from the daily commuting to and from the mines. The hall doubled as a day-care center and school for the children while their parents worked.

The Carters looked around the hall and William had to scout around for a few minutes before locating two empty seats.

Children were not allowed into the hall. They were ushered into a small adjoining room and kept under a company supervisor's eyes. They were all well behaved; those who were old enough had experienced a disciplinary chip at one time. They knew better than to make noise and create disturbances. The younger ones were asleep or too tired to be active.

Exactly on schedule, a man walked up the raised platform in the front of the hall. He held his hands up before him for silence.

"Place your identity cards into the slots in the arms of your chairs," he said.

The miners shifted their weight or stood up to retrieve their cards. William removed his from the side zipper pocket of his orange thermalsuit. He inserted his card and watched as Sandy did the same. A few moments later, when the shuffling and readjusting had died down, the man on the platform called out several names. One person responded and stood up. The person on the platform asked the man where his card was, then cautioned him against going anywhere without it. Admonished, the miner sat down. No one else responded.

Two guards with automatic weapons strode into the hall and down the aisle. Each occupied a front corner. Two more followed them in and occupied the rear corners. William looked around, puzzled, trying to figure out what the guards were for.

The man on the platform raised his hands again to quiet the talking.

"Those men are here for our protection. If you pay close attention to what I say, everyone will be all right. If I say something you do not understand, press the red button in the arm of your chair. I will stop and explain."

William was confused. If this was a regular company meeting, then what were the guards for?

"I will go through this once," the man said.

He stopped and pressed a finger to his ear, and William realized he was listening to someone. The man repeated those names which had gotten no response. No one spoke up. The man nodded once, then cleared his throat.

"Employees of the Morrison Mining Company: due to a bad quarter, missed production quotas, and the drop in market prices for raw materials, the Morrison Payroll Division has ordered all notes due. Payment hours will be from 9:00 A.M. until 12:00 noon. If your debts are not paid by noon, you will be required to attend an emergency meeting here at 1:00 PM. Attendance for that meeting is mandatory for all those who still owe money."

The noise had begun again as the miners turned to one another to talk. The man waited, arms crossed, while the guards raised their weapons. This action alone was sufficient to restore some order.

"Quiet!" the man shouted.

They were quiet.

"It is important you pay attention as I will go through this only once."

74

He paused. No one spoke.

"Payment may be made in cash, Galactic Drafts, company script, uncashed pay vouchers, savings accounts, stocks, or any other valid form of exchange with the following exceptions: jewelry, clothing, or other personal articles. No art objects."

William glanced at Sandy. She was nodding her head slowly, staring at the nape of the person's neck seated before her.

"Remember the meeting at 1:00 P.M. tomorrow."

The man walked off the platform and the guards followed him out. Slowly, life returned to the miners. Discussions started and then quickly burst into a torrent of questions, statements of disbelief, and hysteria aimed at one another. William looked at Sandy again.

The man on William's right tapped him on the shoulder.

"What are you going to do?" the man asked.

William had never seen the man before. "I don't know. I don't know what any of us can do. Can you pay?" William asked.

The man shook his head. "You?"

"No," William said.

The miner stood up slowly, as if it were an effort. "Well, we had it pretty good for a while."

William nodded then turned back to Sandy. He touched her arm and she faced him. "Are you ready to go?"

She shrugged. "Where to? Home to pack?" she asked sarcastically.

William did not smile.

He stared at a sprayed concrete wall for several seconds, then blinked. It was an alley of some sort and there was little light. He felt a tapping on his back and he wheeled around, the surge of adrena-

lin preparing him for fight or flight. Sherman saw
the scarred man motion to the back of his neck

He pushed Ceros-Livingston's neck forward and
saw the white chip's edge. He pulled it out. The
scarred man sounded like he was dying. It reminded
Sherman of what his parents had gone through. He
took pity on the man and searched his pockets. He
found two things of importance: a capsule of poison
and the small, plastic case.

It snapped open with a slight pressure from his
thumb. He placed the white chip in the foam-lined
recess, memorizing its location.

He stood up, slipped the capsule of poison in his
top pocket for possible future use, then changed his
mind. He bent down and placed the capsule in the
scarred man's mouth. He straightened back up and
walked around for a few moments, testing the new
body for injuries or handicaps. There were none.
The body was a little hungry, though.

The scarred man's breathing became very shallow.

That must have been close, Sherman thought.

He tried to remember the last time he had been
aware. He flexed his hands and nervously shifted
his weight from one leg to the other. The scarred
man's body made a gurgling noise, then stopped
breathing. Sherman knelt over and felt for the nonex-
istent pulse. The man's mouth fell open and the un-
dissolved capsule fell onto the concrete floor.

Sherman looked up and down the alley, trying to
get his bearings. Maybe there was a note, something in his pockets. He felt the sides and back of the
plastic suit, then dug into the pockets, emptying
them on the floor.

Change, a stale package of imicigs, a set of keys,
an identity card, several hundred dollars in cash,
credit cards, a chip with a broken corner, and a
newsfiche. Sherman shook his head.

The last he remembered, he was standing under the ramp at the spaceport on Lanta 1 in a woman's body.

He glanced at the identity card. It showed a picture of a man with long, blond hair. The heavy-lidded eyes drooped downward. He looked at the name and address.

KENNETH HANSON
107 W SUB 3 T-7
ALSIS, IXORA
LANTA 2 IND.

Then he was on Lanta 2—an independent. Hanson must have come to help. But what was the situation? Each time he had been inserted in the past, there had always been someone there to explain what was expected of him. Or another of his chips in a different body had made the switch.

All that had to be done was to get the main chip, the one that had been inside Ceros-Livingston, reinserted. That chip held all the recent memories. But even if he removed himself from Hanson to make room for the other chip, the task would not be accomplished. It would leave Hanson with a chip in his hand and no idea of what was expected of him. And then what would Hanson do? Did Hanson know the white chip that had to be reinserted?

Maybe the dying man had told Hanson which chip it was before the exchange.

No, that didn't make any sense at all. Dammit.

He realized he couldn't take the chance of having Hanson reinsert the main chip. Hanson might insert any chip. Or none at all. It was far too risky.

He doubted if remaining in the alley with Ceros-Livingston's body was safe, even for a short period of time. He stuffed Hanson's personal articles back

77

into his pockets and took everything from the dead man but his identity card.

There was no time to feel remorse for the man.

After all, thought Sherman, I didn't kill him. Morrison did.

help take his mind off Walters-Meyer and Sherman. The image of the broken window at the drug shop was still clear in his mind. Philip Sewel-Tarkington had not been a pretty sight.

He knew that thousands of miners working for him died each week, but he never had to see their bodies. When Sherman had destroyed Delat 10, the surviving staff had sent holograms. Morrison had looked at the carnage but was unaffected. Their bodies were like mannequins, limbs twisted out of shape, faces a mask of contorted ecstacy. The idea had been horrifying—not the bodies.

When the holograms from the mining towns on Altair 4 had arrived, Morrison looked at the bodies calmly, coolly, detached, safe and secure in his assumption that Sherman was insane. After Rigel 3, Morrison did not look at any more holograms.

The ones who died in the mines, the ones who died in the barracks; they showed up only as numbers, statistics on a sheet of plastic, an ultrafiche report handed to him weekly by Andra. He reviewed each tally, measuring and balancing recruitment against deaths, juggling the economics of his mining system. It was not until the fifth planet Sherman destroyed that basic economic factors came into play. He stopped looking at the ultrafiche and began looking at the holograms again.

But Philip Sewel-Tarkington was another matter. It was the first time he had seen a body of a man who had been murdered. He had never seen the lump that remained when someone jumped from a tower, or the ghostly white pallor of someone who slashed his wrists, or the exploded bones and flesh of someone shot with a projectile or laser pistol.

Media services and local authorities kept files filled with holograms of murder victims. Morrison had seen some on the holocube and those of his own miners. But seeing a body lying in a pool of blood a scant meter away from the toes of his polished, hand-sewn shoes was a new and revolting experience for him.

"Where are we going?" Andra asked.

"Just walk," Morrison answered.

Their walk home had been slow, almost leisurely. William slipped an arm around Sandy and they strolled together feeling closer than they had for a long time. There were questions that had to be asked, plans that had to be made, but William said nothing.

There was nothing to say.

The front door, keyed to their voices, slipped open as they approached. They entered their home. It looked different to William; it looked sterile, uninviting. Sandy went directly to the thermostat to insure it was still functioning normally.

"Well?" William asked.

"It's okay."

She peeled off her thermalsuit and sank into a chair. The vinavelvet cushion sighed as trapped air escaped through its seams.

William removed his suit, too, and looked around the living room. There was something about the house that bothered him—something he hadn't noticed before.

"You hungry?" she asked.

"No."

"You want to talk now?"

"What's there to talk about?" he asked.

"Getting the hell out of here."

William shook his head. His stomach was unsettled. "It's impossible."

"Really? Two hours ago it wasn't impossible. Two hours ago you wanted to leave as much as I did," she said softly.

"I still do, Sandy, but be realistic. We don't even know what the company has in mind. We should at least see what they plan to do."

She shifted her weight in the chair, increasing the distance between them. William felt she had angled her body away from him.

"I'll go myself," she said.

"No you won't. You couldn't make it."

She took a deep breath and let it out in a sigh. "It doesn't matter anymore. I can't live like this."

William smiled, trying to regain his composure. "Sandy, you're overreacting to the situation a little, aren't you?"

She sat up straight. "What would you like me to do, lie down and let them march all over me?"

William drew his hand back, but the blow never landed. His hand dropped to his lap. He immediately regretted his action.

"Well then, what are we going to do?" Sandy asked.

"I don't know yet. It would be easier to figure out if I knew what the company had in mind."

"Then we wait and see," she said, disgusted.

"Don't make it sound like that. What else can we do?"

"Something. Anything. Put on our thermalsuits, steal some food, money, maybe a weapon, and try to get to the spaceport."

"Where the guards will stop us and send us back."

"Maybe," she said, "but how much more trouble could we be in?"

William wished he had an answer for that. "I don't know, but there are two ways we can find out."

"When you decide which way you want, come upstairs. I'll be in the bedroom."

He watched her walk up the stairs. He sat there, weighing the odds for a successful trek to the spaceport. Surely other families must be considering the same thing.

There must be entire families bundling up against the sub-zero temperatures of the summer night. Little children wrapped in two layers of thermalsuits and boots, little heat generators strapped around their waists for added protection, small packages of food strapped to their backs, setting off on a journey through a night that never should have been.

It was insane. Why would the company call all debts due? No one was foolish enough to believe that production story.

William sat back on the couch and placed his hands behind his head. He watched the patterns of light on the muralwall shift; the colors were soothing, the flow of designs symmetrical, logical.

There must be families who were panicking, too. Going over budget records, talking nervously to desk computers, furiously scribbling notes and numbers onto plastipaper in an attempt to make the numbers lie. But the numbers would lie only to the people— not to the company. The Payroll Division's computers would not be fooled by inept amateurs. People trying to send messages to friends for help—any kind of commitment to aid in making payment—all stopped by either time differential, or more likely, William thought, the company.

He looked around the living room; it was as if he were seeing it for the first time. He knew what was different about it now, what he had never noticed before: nothing in the house was theirs. Nothing. It had all been there when they had arrived.

He understood and rushed upstairs to tell Sandy. She was sitting on the bed, a pillow sandwiched between her back and the wall, reading. He told her what he had discovered and she laughed.

"Of course the company did it deliberately. But

83

you're wrong about the house. We've bought plenty of this furniture. Remember our credit?"

William was unconvinced at first, but after she named several things in the living room, he realized he was wrong. He shook his head, more upset than ever. The company had planned the entire trap. He went back downstairs to try and figure out the difference in the house.

They passed an eatery. Morrison was not in a mood to do anything but eat. Thinking made him worry, worrying made him nervous, and when he was nervous he ate.

The door irised open for him and he walked into a small reception area large enough for twelve people. A small pedestal rose from the carpeting. Morrison read the sign on its face and pressed the number corresponding to the number of his party. The pedestal sank from sight as the doors before him swung open. They entered a smaller, second room and sat down at the table. The smoked glass top cleared to display a menu before each of them.

After they ordered, the lights in the room dimmed and the walls became transparent. The room was moving slowly around the plaza, past the shops and entertainment.

"Nice place," one of the bodyguards said.

"Yes, it is," Morrison said condescendingly.

To Morrison it was just another cheap restaurant. He had eaten in nicer places on poorer planets.

"Andra?"

"Yes?"

"Do you think Walters-Meyer can catch him?"

"I don't know, Mr. Morrison."

He nodded, realizing it was a stupid question. She had been working for him for eight years and not once had she offered an opinion. He wondered why he still continued to ask her. He wished Bobbi was sitting next to him. She would have told him.

Their food arrived and he applied himself to the task with a vengeance, like a little boy in a candy store. Andra ate more slowly.

Morrison's stomach hurt and he tried to ignore the pain. Thinking about it only made it worse. The ulcer which had developed over the years had been unavoidable; it had come with the territory. He reached into his jacket for a pill to ease the burning. He saw Andra watching and knew she would never say anything.

"Where do you think your boss is right now?" he asked one of the bodyguards.

"I don't know, sir, but I can get in touch with him if you like."

"Do that."

The man reached into his pocket and withdrew the flattened disk. He spoke into it and waited for a few moments.

"Mr. Walters-Meyer is on level two, sir. They're organizing a search."

"Let me speak to him."

The man handed Morrison the disk.

"What have you found out?" Morrison asked.

"We found his body," a tinny voice said.

"Where was it?"

"In an alley behind the drug shop. There was an identity card on it: Ceros-Livingston."

"That mean anything to you?" he asked Andra.

She shook her head.

"All right. Meet us in front of the drug shop in fifteen minutes."

"Right."

He returned the disk to the bodyguard. "Let's get going."

As they stood up, the room's walls opened and

the lights came up. Andra inserted a card into the slot in the table to pay. The door opened. They were in the same spot in the plaza as when they had entered the eatery.

"How'd we get back here?" one of the body-guards asked.

Disgusted, Morrison shook his head and began walking.

"We never went anywhere, stupid," his partner said.

They headed for the rendezvous in silence.

Morrison wished he was aboard his yacht with Bobbi. She not only knew what to do to excite and please him, she also really liked him. The only person on the planet he could trust was Andra, and she would never really talk to him. She was always too aware of her place. Andra wouldn't tell him what he wanted to hear, but then again she would never really voice an opinion. And Helene was nothing but trouble. He should have done something about her long ago; perhaps it was not too late.

But Bobbi was different. She was soft when he needed soft, hard when he needed hard. He never had to tell her, either. She wasn't just responsive to him—she had her needs, too. She was moody at times and sometimes bitchy. If he said something to upset her, Bobbi would let him know. There were times when talking to her was worth all the little digs and sarcasms from Helene.

Bobbi listened to him. And if he did ask for her opinion, she always asked for more information before giving a carefully considered answer. Perhaps they were not the most insightful, clever answers, but he could count on her to tell him what she really thought.

Someone bumped into Morrison and the guards quickly grabbed the man. They spun him around and examined the back of his neck. He did not have a receptacle, and satisfied, they apologized and let him go. Morrison wished he had taken two more men along.

Walters-Meyer was waiting in front of the drug shop. The glass and blood had been cleaned up, the body removed, and the front window replaced.

"Where are the rest of your men?" Morrison asked.

"I've got them spaced around the plaza. They're to notify me immediately if they spot anything peculiar."

Morrison nodded. "And the spaceports?"

"Your men have arrived. I got a call from them about ten minutes ago. They said they were all set up."

"Good. Where's Sherman's body?"

"The authorities took it. The head of the force, Colonel Peterson, seemed upset. He said he wants to talk to you."

"Can't you handle it?"

"I tried, but he said he wanted you."

"How did he die?"

"Sherman?"

"Of course Sherman."

"I couldn't tell. Not poison—that much is for sure. It looks like he just died."

"All right. Keep the surveillance in the plaza as best you can. I don't expect miracles from you, Walters-Meyer. As a matter of fact, I don't expect very much at all." He turned to Andra. "Let's go. Pick two semi-intelligent sides of beef to act as bodyguards." He turned back to Walters-Meyer. "Keep in touch with the men we take with us. I'll want to know where you are at all times."

"Right," Walters-Meyer said.

Morrison detected something false in the man's

voice. It wasn't exactly resentment, but there was an undercurrent that should not have been there.

Boring. There was no other way Bobbi could describe it. With Alex and most of the staff and guards on the planet, there was no one left aboard the yacht to talk to.

She tried to spend most of her time alone in her cabin. She listened to tapes, watched the holocube's local broadcasts, played some of the medium-to-difficult computer games, ate alone, paced the room, but there was a limit. A feeling was building inside her, gnawing away.

It was not that she was imprisoned; Alex had told her before he left the ship that she could go anywhere she liked. But Helene was out there, and Bobbi did not want to do much onboard exploring. She had confined herself to her own cabin.

But as the boredom increased, the anxiety increased.

She had to get out of the cabin.

Most of Alex's men had gone and Helene had stayed clear of the lounge while they had still been onboard. She figured that Helene did not like to mix with the employees.

Bobbi's self-containment hadn't even lasted a day.

She pressed the touchplate on the bulkhead near her door.

Just walking down the passageway made her feel better. She saw a single crew member walking in the opposite direction, several meters ahead. When he looked up and saw her, his eyes widened and he smiled. But when recognition dawned, he quickly averted his eyes.

She was a beautiful woman; her Asian features proved a strange, alluring mixture from her Chinese father and Japanese mother. She smiled at him and continued down the passageway toward the lounge, wondering what warnings the captain had given his crew about her. Maybe it was Alex who had said something.

She hadn't seen him for a week.

The door to the lounge slid open and Bobbi walked in. Helene was sitting in a chair, sipping from a tall, frosted glass. Bobbi was surprised to see her and immediately regretted her impulsive decision to leave her cabin.

"Come in, Bobbi," Helene said, looking at her as if appraising a piece of jade. "I'm glad to see you up and around."

Up and around? "Thank you, Mrs. Morrison. How are *you* feeling?"

Helene's eyebrows rose and a faint smile appeared on her lips. Bobbi thought the surgeons hadn't done as good a job as they could have. Helene's skin looked like it was stretched across her face like a layer of latex. Small, sharp wrinkles, like papercuts, appeared around her eyes. It looked like she was wearing a mask.

Bobbi sat down near Helene, trying to look relaxed and comfortable.

"Drink?" Helene asked.

"What are you having?"

"Oh, it's a special drink."

"I'd like to try one."

Helene motioned to the bartender, and Bobbi thought she detected a slight tremor in her upraised arm.

"I'm feeling fine," Helene said.

Bobbi smiled and leaned forward. "Most people have some kind of reaction when they get into space. It's very strange. Some get nervous. I know I get nervous. Without knowing that the ground is underneath me, or even being able to see the ground, or having the stability of some structure connected to the ground, I get edgy."

Helene nodded. "I know what you mean."

"Other people get physically ill, though I'm sure it's only psychological."

"Oh?"

"Yes. Psychosomatic symptoms resembling sea-sickness. With the gravity systems on, there's no disturbance to the inner ear. It's just that they expect to be ill, so they are."

Helene took a long pull from her drink. "Well what do you know."

The bartender crossed the room and handed Bobbi her drink. She tasted it. "What's in here?"

"Just some mixers, flavoring, alcohol, and Mesca-nol."

Mescanol. No wonder Helene looks so tired. "It's good," Bobbi said, taking another small sip. Bobbi had experienced Mescanol on one of Alex's extended visits.

He had brought a small vial of the clear liquid and mixed a few drops in with their drinks. It was a pleasant experience—a mild hallucinogen when taken in small doses, but with frequent and repeated use, its effects became cumulative.

"Have you heard what's happened?" Helene asked.

"No."

"Sherman has gotten away from them again. Alexander sent for the guards to cover the spaceports."

Bobbi was surprised to hear a change in Helene's tone of voice when she talked about Alex and Sherman. It became hard, almost emotionless.

"Oh."

"You don't care very much," Helene said.

"I care."

"You certainly don't show it."

"I didn't realize I had to show it." Bobbi rose and put her drink down on the table by her chair. "It's been nice talking with you, Mrs. Morrison."

"Call me Helene."

"Fine, Helene."

"After all, we have a lot in common."

Bobbi smiled a tight-lipped smile and walked into the passageway.

Me? Like her? Oh, God, I hope not. Alex must know I'm not like her. If I was, why would he bother with me? He's already got one Helene. And one Helene is enough.

She shuddered and hurried back to her cabin.

As hard as he tried, William could make no sense of the line of thought he was following. There couldn't have been anything different about the house. How could he have gotten sidetracked into this dead end? He had to figure out what was happening.

He backtracked and went through it again.

It all stemmed from the feeling he had about the house. There *was* something different.

He sighed and watched the muralwall. It did not soothe him this time. And what about Sandy? The situation around them was becoming worse, yet instead of helping him figure out what to do, she was upstairs, lying in bed, reading.

He scanned the room as carefully as he could.

The warmth *was* gone. But it wasn't the house itself; it had to be Sandy.

8

Sherman found a door at the end of the alley. through a small window in its center he could see a service droptube. He reached into his pocket for the set of keys, looked them over, and tried one that looked right. It fit. Hanson really prepared himself, Sherman thought as the door slid open.

He stood in front of the tube and leaned in. The tube reached upward for twenty, maybe thirty meters. It dropped farther than that. He jumped in and grabbed a handhold. His body was immediately weightless, and as he yanked on the handhold, he began to rise. When he reached the third level he stopped his upward momentum and swung out of the tube. He followed small signs on the alley's walls to the exit. He had to use the key twice.

The last door opened onto a small terrace near a walkway. The third level of the plaza had fewer shops, but more entertainment, hotels, apartments, and restaurants than other levels. He strolled along calmly, irresolutely searching for someone with a receptacle.

"Kenny!"

Sherman continued to walk. He felt a hand on his shoulder, then wheeled around.

"Kenny Hanson! I didn't think I'd see you for a while."

Sherman smiled at her. She was almost his height —just a few centimeters shorter. She had long, wavy brown hair and her eyes were made up so they seemed to sparkle. She was smiling, and Sherman smiled back involuntarily. He felt himself warm to her; she was so alive, so vibrant.

"Hello," he said.

"Kenny, what's wrong?"

"Wrong?" And then Sherman realized he had been daydreaming. She knew Kenneth Hanson— not him. He would only make himself vulnerable by responding to her. She must have easily sensed the difference. "I've just been to Elando's Drug Shop. Down on the first level."

"You? Hmmm." She looked him up and down, smiling, as if reassessing him.

"Just to blow off a little tension. I guess I'm still a little disoriented."

"You sure are." Her smile faded. "I'd say you're so disoriented that you're lying to me."

"Who, me?"

"You can't take drugs. Remember the traumas, or was that just another story?"

A fine sweat broke out on his forehead. He didn't

know who she was or what she wanted. He didn't have the time or the patience to deal with her right now. He didn't even know what the situation with Morrison was. If he could get her name, he could deal with her more easily.

"Come on. I'll buy you lunch and explain the whole thing."

"You're going to buy me lunch?" she asked incredulously. "That's a good one."

"Come on. I'm serious."

She looked him over again, then shrugged. "All right. This is going to be interesting."

Not if I can help it, Sherman thought. She was attractive and she did appeal to him, and it had been a long time, but there were pressing matters that had to be resolved first.

"Well?" she asked, waiting.

"Fine." He took her arm and strolled along with her; the hope of immediately finding a receptacle for the chip with the current memories was gone. The pressure of her forearm against his side felt good. Too good. "How about here?"

"Well, well, well. A real sport. The last time you treated it was soy."

"From now on, it's nothing but the best," Sherman said, carried away, almost immediately regretting it. If and when Hanson got back his body, he would be in a difficult position with this woman. Unless Sherman told her what was happening. "Just do me one favor."

"What's that?"

"You remember how and where we met, don't you?"

"Of course."

"Then tell me."

"Don't you remember?" she asked.

94

"Please. Just tell me."

"We met at a Lanta 3 meeting. Hey, what is this?"

"Never mind. It's going to be okay."

"What's going to be okay?" she asked, irritation coming through in her voice.

He unzipped the suit pocket with his left hand and unsnapped the small, plastic case. He located the right chip by feel, removed it, snapped the case shut, and kept his hand in his pocket.

"Let's get inside. I'm hungry and we can talk there."

She gave him half a smile and followed him into the restaurant. He rubbed the edge of the smooth piece of plastic in his pocket with his fingertip.

"Party of two," Sherman said.

A door irised open and he led the way to the table. The small dining room was just big enough for the centrally located table. The walls were holograms of a rain forest on some planet Sherman did not recognize. The vegetation was strange but not threatening.

"I know you're not Kenny," she said, sitting down across from him. "It's obvious."

"Oh?"

"Just by what you do and say—it's not Kenny at all."

"How does he talk?"

"Who are you?"

"Does it matter?"

"It does to me. I like Kenny."

Sherman perused the menu. The sparkle was gone from her eyes and he wanted to avoid their piercing glare. He looked at the scenery behind her and pointed to a strange clump of orange and fuchsia plants. "Have you ever seen anything like that before?" he asked, left hand ready with the chip.

She did not look. She continued to stare at him. "I could have screamed outside or steered you in the direction of the authorities. They would have questioned you."

"What's your first name?" Sherman demanded.

"Alicia."

"Well, Alicia, I could have killed you. And I may yet. Now turn around."

She did not move. "Tell me who you are."

"My name is Donald Sherman."

He saw her blanch; the blood drained from her face as quickly as a spoonful of water is absorbed by the desert. But there was no fear in her eyes.

She turned around.

He leaned forward with the chip.

It was Thursday morning and there was no work. The chill seemed to linger in the air, and those who went to the Payroll Division to pay off what little they could wore two layers of thermalsuits. It was still summer on Lanta 3.

William and Sandy slept late. There was no reason to get up early. None at all. There was no way they could have paid any of their debt, and as long as they made the 1:00 P.M. meeting, little else mattered.

William watched the portable holoset by the end of the bed. A man dressed in a company uniform sat behind a desk talking, his small form reminding William of marionettes he had once seen as a child on Earth.

"—five families. These families will be dealt with accordingly. The rumor of suicides is completely false. You are not—"

"Suicides?" Sandy asked, sitting up in bed.

"Shhh!"

"—give them any credence. The meeting is still scheduled for one o'clock despite last night's activities. The Morrison Mining Company does not hold these actions—"

Sandy pressed the channel selector in the headboard.

"—but does not consider them a direct assault on personal and company property. As far as work schedules and production schedules—"

She selected a different channel.

"—concerned, one hour will be added each day until the deficiency is made up. As to the attempted escape of payment made by these five families, their trip to the spaceport was not only uncomfortable, but was totally in vain. The guards easily handled the minor disturbance created when—"

Sandy shut off the set. She rubbed her lower lip with her forefinger and eased herself back to the bed.

"What did you do that for?" William asked, leaning over to turn the set on again.

"You heard him, didn't you? How many times do you have to listen to that same shit?"

William stared into the holoset's black cube.

"William?"

"Yes?"

"I'm almost relieved that we didn't go last night. It must have been terrible for those poor people."

"Um hmm."

"Listen to me for a minute."

"I'm listening," he said, still staring into the holoset.

"William?"

He turned and looked at her, feeeling her fear; the warmth that had been missing flooded back. Her nearness made him melancholy. For a few mo-

97

ments it was just he and Sandy, like it used to be. He leaned forward and cupped her face in his hands, pulling her closer. They kissed, then embraced. They held each other tightly until he felt the tears on his arm.

"It's going to be all right, Sandy," he said, trying to believe it himself.

"No, it's not. Don't treat me like a child. Don't tell me it is," she said firmly.

He knew she was right. There was no sense in lying. "Let's have something to eat. Maybe things will look better on a full stomach."

"Wait. I want to ask you something first."

"What?"

"I want you to fight. Fight back. Don't let them take us away like slugs. I want them to know we're people."

"And who am I supposed to fight? Armed guards? The Payroll Division? Morrison himself?" William asked, losing his patience.

"Yes."

"Yes, what?" he asked, almost shouting.

"Everybody, dammit!"

Since the foodwall did not function properly, William and Sandy had to settle for what it would give them. The soy was well flavored and colored, but knowing what it was made it less appetizing.

"You know," William said between mouthfuls, "if we ever get out of this, there's a person I'm going to look up."

"Oh? Who's that?"

"A little man named Benjamin Douglas."

"I should have known," Sandy said, half laughing.

William spent most of the meal thinking about the little man, developing and refining his hate to a fine-tuned irrational vendetta. After all, it was Douglas who had gotten them involved in this whole mess. If it hadn't been for him showing up with that phoney homesteading deal, they would still be on Earth.

"William?"

"Huh?"

"What's the matter? You're not eating. It's not that bad."

"Oh, I know," he said, pushing the soy around with his fork. "I was just thinking about Douglas."

"If it hadn't been Douglas, it would have been someone else," she said.

William forked some soy paste into his mouth, not paying any attention to its color or taste. Instead, he thought about what Sandy had just said. She was right. If it hadn't been Douglas it could have been anyone. Besides, he'd been the one who had been eager to go—homesteading had looked ideal. Then if it wasn't Douglas he was angry with, then it had to be Morrison.

Morrison.

It had to be him. He was the one who owned the whole operation. Douglas and the others like him ran *his* errands. Lanta 3 was his planet. They were his mines. The people, too.

The more he thought about it, the clearer it became.

Sandy placed the trays into the foodwall for recycling, but the accompanying clicks and noises did not follow.

"They've shut it off," she said.

"At least they let us eat lunch."

She laughed. "Surprised?"

He nodded. She sat down again.

"Sandy, I *do* want to fight them. And not Douglas, either."

99

"Welcome back to reality," she said, smiling. She leaned over and kissed him on the cheek. "But you'll never get to Morrison."

"I know that, but if we drag our heels—"

"No. That's not the way. Putting up a struggle won't accomplish anything. I've been thinking about it. We'll probably get killed by some trigger-happy guard. We've got to take our time and look for the spots—then we strike where and when it'll do some good."

"I see what you mean."

"Good. I'm proud of you, Will."

Even with his apprehension over their uncertain future, he felt better. Their plan gave him a feeling of stability—a purpose. And the doubts he'd had about Sandy—whether or not she still loved him— were gone. He felt ready to take on Morrison himself.

Morrison paid little attention to the unassuming chairs, desk, oil paintings, and other clutter in Colonel Peterson's office. He watched the man.

Peterson was slim with a leathery complexion. He had sunken cheeks and, as he stood behind the desk, Morrison thought the man must have been wearing a steel rod along his spine.

"Alexander Franklin Morrison," he said, stepping up to the desk, extending his right hand.

"Sit down, Mr. Morrison. That chair," Peterson said in a cold, controlled voice. He pointed to a large easy chair, ignoring Morrison's proffered hand. "Young lady, would you mind waiting outside?" he asked Andra.

Morrison nodded to her and she left. He slipped his right hand into his jacket pocket.

Peterson sat down, his back remaining perfectly straight. He carefully clasped his hands together on the desk top, then looked at Morrison. "Now, suppose you tell me what's going on."

"You don't need me for this, do you? I'm sure my employee, Walters-Meyer, could have answered your questions. I have a lot—"

"Just answer my questions, please. While you are on Lanta 2 you are subject to all laws, regulations, and—"

"Very well," Morrison said, annoyed.

"Please do not interrupt. All laws, regulations, and customs. To me you are just another citizen."

Just another citizen, Morrison thought. If it wasn't such an insult, it might have been funny. "What do you want?"

"Answer my question. What is going on?"

Morrison shrugged.

"Very well. What are you doing on Lanta 2?"

"Vacationing."

"With a troop of armed men?"

"I like tight security."

"On a vacation?"

"Listen, Colonel Peterson—I don't have to justify my actions to you. I've broken no laws." Morrison leaned back in the chair but, for a man of his size, it seemed small; the discomfort was annoying. "Is there anything else?"

"I had hoped you would cooperate."

"Why? This planet makes criminals welcome— debtors flee in order to escape making payment to my mining company."

"This planet is an independent planet, like many others, Mr. Morrison. I do not set this planet's policies—I only enforce its laws." Colonel Peterson leaned forward. "There have been several incidents since you have arrived on your . . . vacation."

"Oh, really?"

"Our crime rate is normally low. Very seldom do

101

we have any violent crimes. Population density being sufficiently low, not—"

"I understand," Morrison said, right hand sweating.

"Please do not interrupt. The density is sufficiently low that not much of the Behavioral Sink condition, reactions to overcrowding, or ... I see you're tired, Mr. Morrison."

Morrison covered his yawn with his left hand. "Forgive me but I've had a busy day sightseeing."

Colonel Peterson checked his calendar. "Please come by tomorrow at one-thirty, Mr. Morrison. Or should I send a car for you? We can continue our little chat then."

"I'd prefer finishing now."

"Very well, then. What are you doing on Lanta 2?"

"Vacationing."

"Indeed. With your resources? I find it difficult to believe you would select our little planet as a vacation spot. There are some nice resort areas on this planet, but by most standards, they are primitive. Now please cooperate."

"I'm on vacation. The woman sitting in the outer office is my secretary and she would be glad to corroborate my story."

"In that case, Mr. Morrison, I am placing you under arrest."

"Me? What for?" he asked, outraged.

"Murder."

"What? Who am I supposed to have killed?"

"No one. I suspect some connection between you, the death of Ceros-Livingston, and of one of your employees, Sewel-Tarkington."

"Don't try and bluff me, Peterson."

"When you decide to explain your presence at

the plaza where two area-located deaths occurred, we will release you. As for now, I'm afraid I must detain you."

Morrison saw his hand reach for the touchplate on the right side of the desk. He was horrified. The very thought of sitting in one of their detention cells was enough to make his skin crawl. His hand tightened in his pocket. "Wait," Morrison blurted.

Peterson's hand stopped its motion but remained poised, suspended, frozen in immobility. "I'm waiting."

"I came here to find Sherman."

"Who?"

"Sherman! Donald Sherman!"

"I can hear you, Mr. Morrison. Try to relax." Peterson shook his head and moved his hand away from the touchplate. "I'm afraid I find that more difficult to believe than your vacation story."

"I didn't think you'd believe me." He was sweating heavily; his body was soaked. "You're a tool for the independents, Peterson. You believe whatever they tell you to believe."

"My superiors have never mentioned that name. I've heard things about Sherman, but—"

"He's on this planet," Morrison said.

"Oh?"

"Didn't Walters-Meyer inform you?"

"No one from your organization has been in touch with me. Perhaps he spoke to one of my aides..."

Morrison was shocked. Walters-Meyer would have to go. "Perhaps. But whatever you think, Sherman is here."

"Where?"

"We almost had him in the plaza."

"Well, Mr. Morrison, I should inform you of some basic facts. One: Donald Sherman, if he does exist, is a free man while on Lanta 2. Two: you are going to get yourself into more trouble than you can handle by pursuing this matter.

"If, however, he does exist, it would explain this quasi-religious, cult, hero-worship some of the people seem to feel."

"He's here, I tell you," Morrison said. He bit his lower lip. "Make no mistake—the man is real. And he's here."

"Really? What does he look like?"

Morrison tightened his grip on the arm of his chair.

"Are you planning to continue this little escapade?"

Morrison nodded.

Colonel Peterson frowned, then stood. "That's all."

Morrison pushed himself up, ignoring Peterson's outstretched hand. He walked to the outer office, motioned for Andra to follow, then walked out to the aircar. The bodyguards were a few meters away, talking.

Not until they were seated in the aircar did Morrison release the hand clenched around the automatic pistol in his right jacket pocket.

"That bastard," Morrison said.

"He looked like a tough one," Andra said. "Old Interplanetary Monitor."

"He's tough, all right." He took a deep breath and eased back in his seat. He motioned Andra closer and she leaned toward him. "Did you contact Peterson directly, or did you have Walters-Meyer do it?"

"I tried to get through," she said. "Peterson's got more aides than I've run into with anyone. Walters-Meyer offered to take care of it for me when I called him."

The two bodyguards got in the front.

"Take us to the spaceport," Morrison said.

"Alsis?" one of them asked.

"No. Where my shuttle is."

"Tangua," Andra said.

When they were airborne, Morrison felt better, as if he had left his worries behind, on the ground. The distinct change in how he felt made him realize just how tense he had been. That Peterson was a real bastard.

"Walters-Meyer never contacted Peterson," Morrison said softly.

"Is that what Peterson said?" Andra asked.

"Yes."

"And you believe him?"

"Well..."

"I'll keep my eyes open," she said.

"Peterson isn't even sure that Sherman exists."

"I'm not surprised. What else did he say?"

"Just some semireligious shit."

The guards in the front were engaged in their own conversation; Morrison ignored them. He was on his way to his shuttle, and then to his yacht. He would have to make time for Bobbi when he got there.

Let Walters-Meyer chase Sherman for a night, thought Morrison.

"I believe you were in the middle of some apology," Sherman said. In a female voice. It startled him, but only for a moment. It sounded nice in his ears. It was always a jolt when he realized he was in a new body. The man sitting across from him was the man in the alley; long blond hair and drooping eyelids. He smiled at him.

"I'm afraid not. Listen. I didn't know what was happening or where I was. There was no note, no directions—no information for me to go on at all," the Sherman in Hanson's body said.

105

"I see." He looked down to see what he was wearing, caught sight of full breasts and then looked at the Sherman across from him. "Not bad?"

"An attractive body, but more interestingly, a highly perceptive personality with good judgmental powers. Nice, too."

"Right. I'll be nice."

"Thanks. You want me to pull out?"

"May as well."

"Some quick updating for you. I'm Kenneth Hanson. He was well prepared with keys, cash—the whole works. I don't know her full name. Alicia's her first. Find out for me, will you?"

"Sure. Where are we?"

"Third level of some plaza. I guess we're still on—"

"I know the rest. How much time?"

"An hour at most."

"The body?"

"Ceros-Livingston?"

The Sherman in Alicia's body nodded.

"Dead. Died a few minutes after I was inserted."

"Close."

"Yeah. Very close. I'm lucky I took you out before he bought it."

Sherman got to his feet and walked around the table. "We're going to have to update everyone, all at once."

"Yeah," the Sherman in Hanson's body said. "And soon."

"I'll try. The red chip, too. Maybe Handsome will help."

"Cute. It's Hanson."

"Right." He smiled and withdrew the chip from Hanson's neck.

9

William sat on Sandy's right, holding her hand, waiting for the meeting to begin. He was apprehensive but not afraid. They had arrived early, looked around the big, empty hall, and found seats down front.

Other mining families drifted into the hall slowly, quietly, as if attending funeral services. William and Sandy looked over their shoulders at each new arrival. Many looked as though they had not slept; others were tranquil, like bovine creatures being led to market without electric prods.

The meeting was starting and William remained

calm. The company representative strode into the hall and mounted the platform in front of the Carters. He placed his hands firmly on his hips and surveyed the room. William turned around and looked with him. The hall was not quite full; the silence was disturbing.

"Place your cards into the slots in your chair arms," the man on the platform said.

The miners did as they were told.

The man on the platform pressed his finger to his ear. He nodded to some silent direction, then cleared his throat.

"The families missing from this meeting are already in custody. I would advise each of you to cooperate, both individually and as a group, to your fullest capacity from this point on. If you do, you will be rewarded. If you do not, you will be punished," he said.

The doors on both sides of the hall swung open and a contingent of armed guards made its way briskly around the side aisles, surrounding the miners. William turned around in time to see the last guard settle in place at the rear of the hall. No one's going anywhere or trying anything, William thought, puzzled by the appearance of the guards.

"These men have orders to shoot— to fire on anyone who makes what they consider a suspicious move. You are all under company arrest for nonpayment of debts. You are entitled to a trial with representation provided by the Morrison Legal Department for a small fee. If the case is decided against you, court costs will be added to your debt. Does anyone wish to take the matter to trial?"

No one spoke.

William knew what the company was doing was

illegal. Indenturing employees was expressly forbidden by the Interplanetary Monitors. Morrison could never have gotten Lanta 3 with their approval, and continued to sell on the open exchange if they knew about this. He remembered the IM who had walked around the houses just a week ago, making sure that the miners were not taken advantage of. But where was the IM now?

William wondered how many times the man on the platform had gone through the same speech. He actually sounded bored.

"You will follow the guards to Barracks 3. Anyone attempting to leave formation will be shot immediately. If you all remember that the key to a healthy, happy future lies in cooperating and obeying all rules, you stand a better than average chance of regaining the company's faith. Good luck to all of you."

The representative strode off the platform. The guards by the left side door parted to let him pass. A uniformed but unarmed guard near the door took two steps forward.

"Get up quickly and silently," he said. "When you see your children being led down this aisle, follow them out. Those of you without children will wait until the others have left. We will all go through these doors and then outside to where we will all march to the barracks. Remember—these men have orders to shoot."

The miners did as they were told.

As William passed through the doors he took hold of Sandy's hand and gripped it tightly. "Stay by me. Don't get separated."

"I'm right with you," she said.

The guards surrounded the group of miners; one hundred ninety-three families. There was little talking as they walked—only a child's occasional outburst.

"—fault," Hanson said and then froze in fear.

Sherman walked back around the table and sat down opposite the man. "Continue. Your explanation?" Sherman asked, amused by Hanson's obvious disorientation.

"Alicia?"

"Close," Sherman said.

"Oh, I see. What happened?"

Sherman explained what had happened. He finished right after the food arrived.

"I don't like steak," Hanson said.

"Sorry. The chip that was inside you ordered it. I can reinsert the chip and let him enjoy it, or I'll eat it if you like."

"Alicia's a vegetarian."

Sherman shrugged. "Suit yourself."

"I was saying that it wasn't my fault," Hanson said while Sherman ate. "I saw them converge on the bar and realized there was nothing I could do to help. I figured that you didn't need me around at that time."

"Right," Sherman said. "You would have only been in the way."

"That's what I figured. I saw you and someone else come out of the bar. I hung back, and when they followed you into the drug shop, I waited around to see what would happen. The guy you walked in with came crashing through the window —a bloody mess. The others rushed into the shop, then came reeling out. They must have gotten a little of the drug.

"I waited but you didn't come out. Morrison and his henchmen showed up a little after that. Once I found out they didn't get you, I left. I circled around and started working my way through the service alleys and corridors until I found you."

"And just in time, too."

"I guess so."

Sherman could tell that Hanson was unnerved. Whether it was his presence in Alicia's body or Hanson's disorientation from expecting to still be in the alley with Ceros-Livingston, Sherman did not know. Hanson should have gotten over the disorientation by now, though. If it was Alicia, there was nothing Sherman could do about it. He could explain it to Hanson, calm him down, but spending all of his time putting things into their proper perspective for Hanson was not a good idea. But Sherman did need help, and Hanson was his only volunteer.

"What's going on between you and Alicia?" Sherman asked. He saw Hanson wince when her name was mentioned. "It bothers you, doesn't it?"

"Yes," Hanson admitted. "It bothers me a lot."

"That's what I thought."

"She's special."

"That's what he said."

"Who?" Hanson asked.

"The chip that was in your body." He watched Hanson carefully. "Don't worry like that. Nothing happened. And if anything had happened there would be nothing you could do about it—nothing to make things the way they were. If she doesn't do what you want her to do, think the way you want her to think—if her actions don't agree with your expectations of her, find another friend."

Sherman doubted that Hanson would take his advice, but he felt he owed him something; the man had saved his life. If Ceros-Livingston had died while his chip had been inserted, Sherman was convinced he would have died, too. He realized there was little basis for this in scientific fact, but that did not deter him from his belief.

"I want you to find me another body," Sherman said. "I'm not comfortable in a female form."

"Gladly," Hanson said.

Sherman finished eating and tried to ignore the way Hanson furtively glanced at Alicia's chest, over his shoulder, and around the room every few minutes. "Calm down, Hanson. You'll give the whole thing away. Morrison's men aren't stupid."

"Sorry."

"Who's treating?"

"Me." Hanson removed his card and placed it in the slot in the table top. "The organization will reimburse eighty percent, anyway."

"Good. Shall we go then?" Sherman asked, smiling as warmly as he could.

Hanson grimaced.

Morrison was anxious to get back to his yacht and ordered the pilot to take off without proper clearance. The pilot explained that doing this would bar them from ever landing on Lanta 2 again. The pilot could not understand what was holding up their clearance. It should have been routine.

Colonel Peterson called the ship and was put through to Morrison. Two minutes after Morrison explained his intentions of spending a night, possibly several, aboard his yacht, his shuttle was cleared for takeoff.

"He's a tough one," Andra said.

"Indeed," Morrison commented.

The trip to the yacht, though not especially long, was boring. Andra slept.

They walked to the barracks with shuffling feet. The fear was so intense, so real, William could almost smell it. He felt his confidence sag. The guards managed to watch both the miners and the ground before them. The afternoon was cold; William was glad he and Sandy had worn two layers of thermal-suits.

The cement walkways had stopped several meters beyond the meeting hall. There was a path worn in the ground and William could tell from the lack of native vegetation on the path that many had made this walk before him. He wondered how long it would be before the next group of unsuspecting miners were taken into the deceptively open arms of the company, only to be herded off to the barracks like criminals. Like animals.

There was little wind, and the sun offered little warmth.

William sighted a row of long, low buildings about a half kilometer away. He squeezed Sandy's hand and pointed to them; they had always been hidden in the past. The barracks were isolated—too far away to be seen from the housing development, hidden from the stores by a large copse of native trees and bushes, and set in the opposite direction of the mines.

The guards stopped them fifty meters from the barracks, and the same, unarmed guard called for their attention.

"You will be assigned bunks and a locker for any personal possessions you may have with you once we're inside. The perimeter of this area is protected by laser beams to prevent intruders from doing any harm to you or to company property. These beams lack the ability to determine whether someone is trying to enter the area, or leave it. You people with children, make certain they understand.

"The security system will be deactivated each evening when the night shift leaves and when they return one half-hour before dawn. Once you are comfortably located and familiar with the regulations and schedules, you are free to walk around the grounds. Be careful not to stray too far. If any of you has seen someone burned by a laser, please share this experience with your fellow miners. It is important that *everyone* understands.

"I will post the schedule for those who will be working the night shift."

He turned away and the guards started the miners moving toward the long, low buildings. William hoped the security systems had been deactivated—dying as a smoldering ember on the ground of Lanta 3 was not an attractive way to go. And definitely not in his plans.

There were four cement steps that led into Barracks 3. As William and Sandy climbed them, they looked into the building and saw their new home.

The barracks were over one hundred fifty meters long and very narrow. The left and right sides were lined with triple-decker bunk beds almost all the way down the building's length. There were no windows. The narrow aisle that ran down the middle ended in a small sitting area capable of holding about a quarter of the miners. There were tables, chairs, a large board with papers tacked to it, and two doors on either side. William was assigned a bottom bunk about a third of the way down the aisle on the left side. Sandy was assigned the bunk directly over his.

The unarmed guard posted the work schedule in the sitting area and then left with the guards. William was relieved that there had been no incidents during their walk to the barracks. It was not necessary for him to see the guards kill someone to believe they would have done it.

He opened the locker beneath the bunk and read

the instructions on the inside of the door. He set the lock with his thumbprint. He shut it and had Sandy try to open it, to test it. He was surprised to find it worked. Sandy set hers, then sat beside William on his cot.

"This is it," she said. "This is what they planned for us all along."

William looked down to the front wall through the strange multiple frame the cots created. "I don't think this is the end of it," he said. "I wonder where we eat? Do they have bathroom facilities here?"

"We'll find out soon enough," Sandy said.

He watched the other families on their cots, talking to each other. He unzipped his pockets and emptied their contents on the cot. Some of the younger children began crying. William bent down and put his personal possessions in his locker. He slipped his identity card back into his pocket and zippered it.

More children started to cry, afraid of their new surroundings, the large number of people, and sparked off by the others. William tried to ignore the conversations taking place all around him. Privacy is in the mind, he told himself. But he didn't believe it. The more he tried not to listen, the more he heard.

The children screamed.

Benjamin Douglas pushed his glasses back onto the bridge of his nose and smiled at the young couple before him. They looked eager. It was obvious, despite their efforts to appear unenthused. The company paid well for couples that were this young. If he could get them to sign up for that hellhole of a planet, Randu, the bonus would be greater and in his account by the end of the month.

Morrison Mining Company stock had dropped a few points and it was the perfect time to buy.

If he kept it up, Douglas knew he would be able to retire to a recreation section on Earth. Or maybe, if his recruiting luck held, one of the more exotic pleasure planets. It's a good life, he reflected, handing the pen to the young couple.

By the time the docking had taken place, Morrison was nervously exhausted. He got out of the acceleration seat wearily and shook Andra awake. She rubbed the sleep from her eyes while the sterilization procedure took place.

The yacht was quiet.

The crewmen on the night shift went about their business orderly and efficiently. Morrison was relieved to find neither of the women there to meet him. He said goodnight to Andra and set off for Bobbi's cabin.

He pressed the touchplate and her door opened.

"Alex? Is that you?" she asked.

A small light came on near the bed and Morrison took a few steps into the room.

"Thank God you're back. I was getting worried."

He smiled. "I'm all right. Just tired."

"Come on over here and I'll rub your back."

"Not yet, Bobbi. I have to take care of a few things first. I'll be right back."

She got out of bed. The nightgown she wore concealed little. Morrison swallowed. She crossed the cabin and pressed herself against him. Her warmth and softness were too much for him to cope with; he kissed her, then gently broke the embrace.

"I've got some people to check up on. Sherman managed to—"

Bobbi pressed her forefinger to Morrison's lips. "No

business. Not now. Not here. Go take care of whatever you have to, then come back."

He kissed her again, then started to walk out. He stopped by the door and caught her in the middle of a stretch, arms thrown back, erect nipples pressing against translucent whisps of cloth, standing on tiptoes, cascades of black, silken hair falling to her waist. He sighed, stepped out into the passageway, and closed her door.

His suite was around a corner and on the end of the same passageway. He walked in to find Helene sleeping on the couch. When he turned on the light, she sat up slowly. She rubbed her eyes and, as she yawned, he began to undress. He removed a silk dressing gown from a closet and laid it on the bed.

"Did you get him?" she asked, clearing her throat.

"No."

"What happened?" she demanded.

"We'll talk about it in the morning. I'm tired."

"You look terrible," she said.

Morrison pulled the dressing gown around his nude body.

"Have a nice time with her," Helene said.

Morrison gestured with his hand, offering her the bed, smiling. He knew she wouldn't accept his invitation—she hadn't in years. And yet, she was perverse enough to accept, just out of spite. "No?" he asked, trying to keep the contempt out of his voice.

The surgeons should have sewn that up, too, he thought. While they were doing her face.

He walked down the passageway to Bobbi's cabin.

"Hey," William said, grabbing a man by the arm. "What's going on?"

The man stopped and motioned to the sitting area

117

with a jerk of his thumb. "There's a whole sheet of regulations back there, fellow. They're tacked up right next to the work schedule."

William released his grip on the man's arm and looked back to the sitting area. It was too crowded to get back there—the crowd was thick and noisy. "What are they?"

The man shook his head. "You'd better read them for yourself. Damn, if I made a mistake and ended up telling you the wrong thing—" he drew a finger across his throat "—and I wouldn't do that to nobody."

"Thanks," William said. The man walked back to his family, shaking his head as he walked. "I'll go back there when it thins out a little," William said to Sandy.

She was lying on his cot, staring at the bottom of the mattress above her. "They'll probably be strict regulations," she said. "With this many people in such a small place—"

"Yeah," William said.

"It's going to be rough," she said.

"Very." He looked at her, then tried to calculate the width of the cot. It looked like it was a little over a meter wide. He smiled. "Move over."

She slid to the edge of the cot so he would have room. He stretched out beside her and pulled her close, trying to suppress the desire he felt rising. Two children stood at the foot of their bunk, staring with eyes wide. William sat up and stared back until he embarrassed them into moving.

The sounds of uncontrolled hysterics were scattered throughout the barracks, adding to the noise and confusion. William closed his eyes. That was easy. He tried to close his ears.

A couple on his right talked about the terrible lack of privacy and the tremendous din. The man on his left calmly but steadily lectured his children on behavior under these strange conditions. He was trying to make them realize the seriousness of the situation. William thought the man would succeed only in putting more fear and panic into an already volatile situation.

This was not the way to do it, William thought. Make the kids think it's a game—a vacation—anything but the cold, terrifying reality of the barracks. They'll walk around too scared to breathe, and then it'll all come apart at the seams. After a few hours, if they last that long, these kids will be as hysterical as the rest of the children. Panic spreads quickly.

He wanted to tell the father he was making a mistake. He wanted to get up on the top bunk and shout everyone into silence. There were ways the living conditions could be made bearable, but it would take cooperation.

The man and the woman to his right were already involved in a heated argument. William pulled Sandy closer and tried to block it all out.

Hanson and Sherman walked arm in arm, window shopping. They strolled leisurely, stopping to watch the flaming high-wire act in the center of the plaza, then a rally race on jetskis. Sherman felt himself relax for the first time in months. He would have liked it better if he had been in a man's body for comfort; he was not used to being a few centimeters shorter than the people he had to deal with.

More importantly, once in a while Hanson would forget it was Sherman he was walking with. Sherman did not mind when Hanson slid his arm around his shoulder—it was necessary not to stand out. Only lovers strolled this section of the plaza. Lovers or hunters. But then Hanson would forget and lean too close, touch Alicia's body, embrace for an intended kiss. It was at these times Sherman most wished for a male body.

But it was normal for Hanson to do these things.

Other couples around them were much more intimate, and although the contact with Hanson made him uncomfortable, Sherman realized there was little he could do.

They made their way to the underground tubes. Hanson led Sherman into the cars heading for the west sector and Sherman tried not to look like a tourist. The train was quiet and fast. They got off at the second stop.

"Stay close," Hanson said. "This area isn't the best."

"Right," Sherman said.

They walked off the platform and into a corridor. Hanson stopped before the first droptube and held Sherman back. He looked around on the floor until he located a piece of debris. Hanson wadded up the piece of paper and tossed it inside the tube. It was instantly shredded by a sleeting rain of razor-sharp particles.

"We'd better try the next one," Hanson said.

Sherman was confused. "What's that all about?"

"Hunters. Out for cash. They hang up on a level above and as soon as they spot any movement, they cut loose with those homemade guns. The authorities try to catch them, but they haven't been very successful."

Sherman nodded in appreciation.

They repeated the procedure twice in the next droptube just to be sure. Hanson entered first and pushed downward. Sherman waited for a few seconds, then followed. They pulled themselves out on sub 3.

"It's just a short walk from here," Hanson said.

Sherman kept his eyes open and his mind as alert as he could. "Where is everyone?"

"This isn't the kind of place you go wandering around at four in the morning. It's just not considered de rigueur."

Sherman could feel how tired Alicia's body was. His mind was still active and clear, but he was afraid the body might begin to slow him down. They stopped before a door and Hanson inserted his card in the slot. He pressed his thumb to the glowplate and the door slid open.

Hanson stepped aside and made an exaggerated sweeping motion while bowing. "After you, mademoiselle."

Sherman shook his head. "You first."

Hanson shrugged and went into the room. The lights came up.

Two men with sidearms sat facing the door. "Come on in," one of the men said.

Sherman spun around ready to flee. Another man had come up behind him and had leveled a pistol at his chest. There was no choice. He entered the apartment.

10

Sherman disliked guns. Not because they killed—killing was an action with definite ramifications—ramifications Sherman did not fear—but rather because there was no defense against a gun. You can wear nose filters to combat gas, use drugs to counteract chemicals, radiation suits for atomic fallout, hand-to-hand combat for a knife, but at close distance you don't argue with a gun, Sherman thought.

You cannot outrun a laser beam; you cannot put your hand out and stop a metal projectile; falling to the ground and rolling out of the way when instant death was a millimeter away—the distance a trigger had to be pulled—was totally insane.

"What's going on, Kenny?" Sherman asked.

"Have a seat, lady. You Hanson?" the one who had talked before asked. All three men looked alike. They wore steel-gray-colored jumpsuits and were built alike. The one who talked had a deep, resonant voice.

Hanson nodded to the man.

"My name is Hill, Mr. Hanson. Walters-Meyer sent us."

Hanson seemed visibly relieved. "You had me going for a minute."

When Hanson sat down, Sherman decided it was time to press for some information. "Who is Walters-Meyer?"

"Who's she?" Hill asked.

"That's Sherman," Hanson said.

"She's Sherman?" Hill asked. "I've got a message for you, lady."

"Who is Walters-Meyer?" Sherman repeated.

"Our boss," Hill said.

"Morrison's man on Lanta 2," Hanson added.

Sherman took a quick look around the room. Three doors—none of them manual—no windows. Two of the men had laser pistols resting in their laps; Hill held a hard-projectile pistol by his side. There wasn't a chance he could make it. Besides, Hanson still had the small, plastic case in his pocket and there was no way he could afford to leave it. "Thanks, Hanson."

Hanson shook his head. "Relax. What's the message?" he asked Hill.

"Walters-Meyer says he's not sure how much longer he can hold it together. He's had it with Morrison—he says either get Sherman off the planet or he'll have to stop cooperating."

"What else?" Hanson asked.

"He's afraid Morrison may be onto him. I'll tell

123

you," he said in a confidential tone, "there's not much room left to breathe. The strain's tremendous. Morrison went back to his yacht so he's got some time, but not a lot."

Hanson ran a finger through his hair, deep in thought.

Sherman was angry. "What would have happened if I hadn't spotted Sewel-Tarkington? And what about finding the drug shop? What if I hadn't gotten away?" Sherman demanded.

Hill shrugged. "Listen, Sherman—you just take care of yourself. I don't know anything about that. If things worked out, consider yourself lucky. Walters-Meyer didn't have to send Sewel-Tarkington—he could have sent someone with a slot. If Walters-Meyer wanted to get you—" he pointed his pistol at Sherman's abdomen "—it would be this simple."

"Right, I understand," Sherman said. What kind of game was Walters-Meyer playing? His agents seemed bent on catching me in the plaza, Sherman thought, and yet now they couldn't care less.

But at the same time, Walters-Meyer had given him a fighting chance—he hadn't been there to supervise and he *had* sent Sewel-Tarkington, Sherman reflected.

"How long will Morrison be on his yacht?" Sherman asked.

Hill shrugged. "We don't know yet." He got up and motioned to the other men. They rose to their feet and stuffed their pistols inside their jumpsuits. "When you've got something specific, let us know, Hanson. He wants to help while he still can. Nice meeting you, ma'am."

Sherman laughed, and the sound that emerged from his lips was not the laughter of a woman. "Nice meeting you, Hill."

The shocked expression on Hill's face increased Sherman's amusement.

"And you want me to believe that Morrison doesn't know?" Sherman asked, kicking off his shoes.

"He hasn't until now," Hanson said. "We should have time to get a plan together before he's sure of Walters-Meyer."

Sherman yawned. "Good. Right now I need some sleep. Do you have to work tomorrow?"

"No. I have a few weeks off—my boss understands. I'll be with you until you don't need me anymore."

"Good." He stretched out on the couch and locked his hands behind his head. He glanced over at Hanson and saw him staring. "What's the matter? It still bothers you, doesn't it?"

Hanson nodded. "Does it bother you?"

"Get me another body. I already asked you for one."

"I will. First thing tomorrow."

"Fine."

The apartment was small—too small for comfort if Sherman decided to undress. Sleeping in Alicia's clothes was not an appealing idea, but he realized it would be easier for both of them. There was no need to make an already precarious situation more difficult.

Hanson paced around the room for a while, then settled into a chair.

"Aren't you going to get some sleep?" Sherman asked.

"I'm not tired."

"Try," Sherman said as firmly as he could. His voice lacked the power he was used to, though, and he was afraid his control of the situation was rapidly slipping.

Hanson sighed, then stood up. He walked stiffly to the wall by the door and pressed a panel. It slid away to reveal a panel of touchplates. He pressed two and the chairs sank into the floor and a bed appeared. He undressed quickly and lay down.

"Good night," Sherman said.

"Yeah. Good night."

Sherman closed his eyes but did not sleep. He waited until he was sure Hanson was sleeping before he relaxed. He repeated to himself over and over to wake up at the first noise in the room, then fell into a light, fitful sleep.

Sherman awoke with a start when Hanson pulled back the sheet. He sat upright, wide awake, before Hanson's sheet had settled back to his bed. When he realized what the noise had been, he eased himself back onto the couch and watched Hanson walk to the bathroom.

"What time is it?" Sherman asked.

"Eleven-thirty," Hanson replied from the bathroom.

Sherman rubbed his eyes. He was still sleepy; what little rest he had gotten through the early morning hours had not been enough for Alicia's body. This kind of living did not agree with him—abandoning body after body, just when he was getting used to them. Ceros-Livingston had served him well.

"You want something to eat?" Hanson asked, standing before the couch.

"What? Oh, sure. I guess so," he said, sitting up. "The faster you get me a body, the better."

"I'll try to find a volunteer. I should be able to

126

get into a meeting of a cell this afternoon at two. If I can locate it."

"Bring the whole cell here if you do. I want to pick the best one."

"What?"

"You heard me. Bring them all. I have to update the chips, too. You should be in on the planning session, so make sure these bodies are good. Bring back four. And leave me the chips."

"What chips?"

Sherman clenched his little fists. "The chips in the plastic case." Hanson's face showed no recognition. "Check your pocket—the suit you wore last night. When I was in your body, I slipped them into your pocket."

"Oh." He walked across the room to the chair where he had draped his clothes. He felt around in the pockets, withdrew the case, and tossed it to Sherman.

Sherman snapped it open with a slight pressure from his thumb and looked inside. Two white chips and one red one. Good.

"Let's have something to eat," Hanson said. He used the touchplate panel to restore the living-room arrangement. The foodwall was to Sherman's right. Hanson walked over to it and pressed a touchplate, exposing a hole. "Put your hand inside," Hanson said.

Sherman did as he was told and a second later, a tray slid out of a slot to his right. "What's that?"

"All the vitamins, minerals, and nutrients Alicia's body needs right now. It does a chemical analysis, then provides you with an edible mixture."

"Not bad. Not fancy, but not bad," Sherman said.

"I'm sorry it's not up to your standards," Hanson said.

Sherman realized there was no way he could continue to work with Hanson while in Alicia's body. He was tempted to tell Hanson to go out into the corridors and grab the first person he saw with a receptacle—anyone, no matter what their physical condition—just to get out of her.

Too bad, Sherman thought. One of my chips really likes her, too.

Hanson would have turned him in if he could have, but he realized that if he handed Sherman over to Morrison, the whole organization would crumble. And the organization did more than just help Sherman.

Every person who had managed to escape from one of Morrison's mining planets had to go underground for several months to escape immediate retribution. Morrison's men had two months to locate and extradite escaped debtors, thanks to the Interplanetary Monitors. And the IMs were a real joke, Hanson thought.

They made the regulation that prohibited indenturing miners. Morrison pays them off so that when they come for an inspection, everything looks okay. The day after the IM leaves, Morrison ships his people off to barracks, Hanson thought. By the time the IM comes back, there's a new batch of miners occupying the houses. The IM conveniently overlooks the fact that none of the families or faces are the same, then leaves.

And if that wasn't bad enough, the IMs give Morrison two months to locate any escaped debtor. Thank God we've got the underground.

Hanson's parents had taken a tremendous risk when they smuggled him off Lanta 3. Hanson had been placed inside a shipment headed for Lanta 2. Luckily, the freight cabin aboard the shuttle had been pressurized and his parents had guessed the destination of the shuttle correctly. He had never found out if his parents had been punished for their actions, and he would never place them in further jeopardy by trying to contact them.

He remembered he was met at the spaceport by a woman. She had been in the underground and, while supervising the unloading operations, had hurried him out of sight and hidden him for four months. She took him to a meditech who examined him and said the chips had done little if any damage. But there was no way for the meditech to remove the receptacle without doing damage; he was not that skilled.

As Hanson grew older, he realized how lucky he had been. The woman died a few years later and, except for the organization, he was alone.

When he had volunteered to help Sherman, to be the one to serve as a contact, it had been a spur of the moment decision. He realized that Sherman helped their cause and, although his actions were violent, they were understandable. To a degree. It was not the most pleasant philosophy Hanson had heard, but it did work. And everyone in the underground seemed willing to wait for its results.

As he floated down the droptube to sub 7, Hanson thought how different it was from what he had expected—with Sherman real, alive, breathing in Alicia's body. He hadn't minded giving Sherman the use of his own, but knowing he was in her was distressing.

The flashing red light alerted him that sub 7 was just ahead. He readied himself, prepared to grab the silver handholds.

He knew the cell would not be expecting him and that there was a chance they would try to kill him before he could properly identify himself. But he knew he had to take that chance. His superior had made it clear that Sherman was to get whatever he wanted.

He had never thought that would include Alicia.

Hanson grabbed the handholds and swung himself out of the tube and into the corridor. It was worse on sub 7 than it was on sub 3. The overhead lighting panels were dimmer, yellower, and the whole atmosphere was depressing. The hallways were run down. He was alert as he walked.

Sherman would be all right in the apartment. No one was expected—Hanson was supposed to be away on vacation.

He knocked on the cell leader's door. A voice asked who it was and Hanson identified himself. They went through the ritual of passwords and codes until, at last, the cell leader opened the door. It took little time for Hanson to explain the situation. He could see none of the men were eager to go with him.

"This isn't a club you belong to," he said, addressing the small group. "You all understood the aims of the organization when you joined."

"In theory," one of the men said.

Hanson understood what the man meant only too well; it had been the same for him. "This is your opportunity to put your theory into practice. If you don't, then what good are you?"

"Hey, now wait a minute—"

"No, *you* wait a minute. There are no shades of gray in this situation. You're either with the organization, or you're not." Hanson stood. "I'm leaving now. Is anyone coming?"

The men looked at each other and, grumbling like old men on their way to visit the doctor, followed Hanson to the door.

Sherman searched the apartment quickly and efficiently, not knowing how long Hanson would be. He found nothing out of the ordinary and was more apprehensive about this than if he had found something illegal. It seemed as if Hanson had no secrets.

Sherman stood in the center of the room, taking in the apartment's general appearance. It was not especially homey in either decor or mood, and he had trouble imagining what kind of man would live like that. It wasn't spartan, but it was devoid of personality. The furniture was functional, but not consistent in style; the walls were a plain, ordinary off-white, devoid of paintings or any kind of decoration; there was no unifying color or sense of complimentary color scheme. The longer he looked, the more convinced he was that something was wrong. Hanson was too good to be true.

Any man who lived so simply, so plainly on the surface, must be hiding something down deep, he decided. He had seen it before—men who were one thing and tried to be something else. Those who were good at it, the professionals, created secondary personalities with quirks in order to mislead. But Hanson was not that good. He should have left something around the apartment to show he was human, Sherman thought.

He realized he was foolish in placing his trust in this man.

It had been a momentary softening, a weak position, and Sherman hoped it was not too late to rectify the situation. He had bent too far to avoid hurting Hanson's feelings and, in doing so, had played into his hands.

Sherman shook his head and sighed, tired.

He felt gritty and uncomfortable from spending the night on the couch fully clothed. He felt around on

Alicia's clothing for a seam, zipper, or some sort of fastener, but found none. Sherman laughed softly, amused to find himself doubly trapped; once in the apartment, and then in Alicia's clothes.

He went to the closet and removed one of the jumpsuits that hung there. He hoped it would fit, that Hanson's taste in women was as unidirectional as it appeared to be.

He tore the dress from his body. She wore no undergarments. Naked, the chill of the air conditioning washed over his body, erected Alicia's nipples, sending sensations through his body. He rubbed their hardness as he walked toward the bathroom.

The mirrorwall showed him her body—full, unsagging breasts, shaved pubic area, nicely shaped legs and waistline. He stopped rubbing her breasts. It felt too good. He decided to clean up first, then let his hands stray over her body. He stepped into the cleaning unit.

After the unit had cleaned him, he walked up to the sink. He checked the cabinet behind the small mirror in front of him for mouthwash, trying to block the image that looked back at him from the polished steel surface.

It was funny, he thought as he rinsed his mouth. Of all the bodies and sex shops I've been in, this is the first time I've been aroused in almost a year.

He turned around and faced Alicia's reflection in the mirrorwall behind him. I owe it to myself, he decided. He turned back to the sink, shut off the running water, and slipped the jumpsuit on.

Hanson stopped before the door and inserted his card into the slot. He pressed his thumb to the glowplate. While the door slid open, he turned and faced the men behind him. "Wait here and I'll be back to get you," he said. "I want to make sure he knows it's us."

He walked into the apartment and glanced around, looking for Sherman. He saw the light from the bathroom and walked up to the doorway. Hanson saw Sherman in Alica's body standing before the mirrorwall, fully clothed, staring at her reflection.

"Sherman?" Hanson said.

Sherman turned calmly, not at all surprised by Hanson's presence. "Did you get them?" he asked.

Hanson nodded.

"Did you bring them inside?"

"No. They're waiting out in the corridor."

"Good," Sherman said. "Come in here for a moment."

Hanson walked into the bathroom, heart pounding, not knowing what to expect. He stopped about a meter away from him. Sherman closed the distance in a single, fluid, catlike movement and slipped his arms around Hanson's neck, kissing him. Hanson was revolted, and he repelled her, pushing her away. Sherman looked hurt.

"What's this supposed to be?" Hanson asked.

"Everyone gets lonely."

Hanson backed up a step, holding his hands before him. "Well not with me you don't. I'm hetero."

Sherman leered and quickly yanked down the zipper on the front of the jumpsuit. In the same motion, he grabbed a handful of the cloth and pulled it aside to reveal Alicia's rounded breasts.

"What am I?" Sherman asked. "Male? Does this look like a man to you?"

Hanson, though aroused by the sight of Alicia's body, still made no move to approach. "Sherman, no matter whose body you occupy, you'll still be Donald Sherman. Knowing that stops me cold."

Sherman looked dejected and let the strained

material return to its normal position. He rezipped the jumpsuit. He shifted his weight, then covered his eyes. Hanson felt awkward and responsible for Sherman's state. He stepped forward and slipped an arm around his shoulders.

"It might have been different last night," Hanson said. "It was my mistake then, thinking of you as Alicia. But now I know better." He pulled him closer and squeezed him gently. "If only it had been anyone but Alicia, I might have done it."

Sherman seemed not to acknowledge anything Hanson had said.

"Don't you see?" Hanson asked. "It's not you—it's her."

Sherman nodded. Hanson let him go. They walked out of the bathroom together, each walking stiffly, too aware of the other's presence. Sherman eased himself down into a chair. "Tell them to come in," he said.

Hanson walked to the door and let them in.

When Sherman looked up, the men had seated themselves around him. He looked them over and sized them up as nervous, scared types who would much rather be playing poker than playing life. He had an innate dislike for the men.

"You know why you're here?"

They nodded; one said yes.

Sherman stood, retrieved the plastic case, and returned to the group. The cell was larger than Sherman had expected. There were only a total of four chips left: three white ones; one of which was himself, inside Alicia, and two in the small, plastic case; and one red chip. Vladimir's fantasy, he thought.

Despite Hanson's discomfort and request, Sherman did not want to leave Alicia's body yet. The cell consisted of four men. He needed two of them. He would use Hanson, but not as he had originally planned.

"I don't need them all," Sherman said to Hanson. "I've changed my mind. Which two do you want to let go?"

Hanson pointed to two of the men. "These two have families."

"Fine," Sherman said. "I wasn't planning to kill anyone—I just want to update the rest of my chips and do a little planning."

But the men were already on their way to the door as if they had been granted a stay of execution. They left without looking back.

"Turn around," Sherman said.

"Why did you let both of them go?" Hanson asked. "Are you going to continue to use Alicia?"

"Relax, Hanson. I told you this was just an update and planning session." Sherman walked over to the couch and the two men turned their backs to him, baring their receptacles. Sherman removed a white chip and slipped it into the first man. He wheeled around, eyes darting, searching for exits, sizing up the situation. "Relax," Sherman told him. "It's an update."

"Fine," the man said.

Sherman turned toward Hanson. "I'll use him after this session, all right?" he asked, pointing to the man he had just put the chip into.

Hanson nodded.

"Your turn," Sherman said.

Hanson turned around and Sherman slipped the remaining white chip into his receptacle. Hanson wheeled around, repeated the first man's actions.

"You relax, too. It's an update."

"Fine," the Sherman in Hanson said. "How you doing?"

Sherman smiled, relieved to find he had put the

right chip into Hanson, the chip that had been in Hanson before, the chip that liked Alicia. He inserted the red chip into the remaining man.

"Well, we're all here and all aware," Sherman said.

"It's been a long time," Sherman said.

"Yes, it has," Sherman agreed.

Tell them I'm glad they've included me. "I'm glad you've included me," the man with the red chip said. *Thanks.*

11

The Carters, like all the other miners in Barracks 3, were given fifteen minutes to prepare for breakfast. They shuffled and stumbled bleary-eyed down the end of the aisle through the sitting area to the bathroom. In front of chipped basins and fogging mirrors, the miners lined up to wash. Some used the multiple shower stalls.

Families reunited after washing for the march to breakfast. They ate amid constant noise: buzzing conversations about what the day might hold, questions about what to expect. They filed out to the tram apprehensively.

The ride was slow, the cars open, uncomfortable.

William wondered what provisions the company made for inclement weather, then laughed silently. The company wouldn't care once they reached this status. He turned his attention to the slowly moving scenery. The small line of stores and buildings were barely visible through the early morning haze. The grass grew like weeds, in clumps, in earth that was a mixture of brown and gray. Bleak, William thought.

Of all the planets the captain of the pickup ship had offered to set us down on, why did we have to pick Lanta 3? he wondered. Yet he knew the others would have been no better. He shook his head.

"What's the matter?" Sandy asked softly, aware of the others in the crowded car with them.

"Just look at this place," he said, motioning to the passing landscape with outstretched arms. He breathed in deeply, then exhaled slowly. "Kind of takes your breath away."

"I'll take your breath away if you're not quiet," the man next to him said, leaning close and clamping William's forearm in a steely grip.

"I was just kidding around," William said carefully. He did not want to cause any fights; the rules posted in the barracks' sitting room had been explicit about fighting.

The man eased his grip. "Sorry."

The miners in the cramped car tried not to purposely eavesdrop, but William still noticed a lull in the conversations that had been going on around them.

"It's okay," William said. "We're all on edge."

"I guess I lost my sense of humor," the man said. He extended his hand and forced a smile. "My name's Dave. Dave Tanner-Snyder."

William shook the stocky man's hand and introduced himself. The other miners in the car struck up their conversations again, satisfied that the argument was not going to escalate. William introduced Sandy to Dave, and she asked if he was married.

"I'm not sure," he said. "Some bastard put my wife and me on separate shifts. I haven't seen much of her over the last twenty-four hours."

Sandy winced. "Have you told anyone about it?"

"I tried, but no one wants to listen. The guards gave me a runaround. The one person I found who looked like a supervisor just shrugged and said there was nothing he could do about it."

"Any children?" William asked.

"No. You?"

"No. I guess we're lucky on that account," William said.

"Don't like kids?" Dave asked.

"No, it's not that," he said, glancing at Sandy. "I'm glad we aren't bringing up any new miners for Morrison."

They were silent for a few moments, listening to the steel wheels roll over the tracks.

"You think he knows what it's like?" Dave asked, elbows on his knees, head cradled in his palms. "I mean really knows."

"Who?"

"Morrison."

William shrugged.

"He knows," Sandy said. "He knows."

William had been waiting for the tracks to swing around the base of the hill to the entrance he was used to entering the mine through, but they did not. The tram entered through an old, outdated adit, and he was surprised. "A different mine?" he thought aloud.

"Could be," Sandy said.

Her noncommital and disgruntled tone disturbed him, but he suppressed the urge to ask what was bothering her. Too many people around and a couple three seats up were already engaged in a bitter, petty argument. No matter how slight the problem actually was, William realized it would sound worse to an outsider. Things were strained enough without adding to the tension.

The tram entered the hill.

The lighting inside the tunnel was poor, and though he couldn't be sure, he thought he caught a glimpse of a man every few meters, standing against the tunnel wall. When he tried to look directly at them, they were difficult to detect. Dark clothes, spaced at five-meter intervals—guards, William decided. Armed guards in the mines? He nudged Sandy and motioned toward them.

"What?" she asked, not understanding.

He leaned close and, in a low voice, told her what he saw. She watched for a few moments, then spotted one.

"Why?" she asked softly.

He shrugged.

The tunnel emptied into a large, high-ceilinged chamber. The tram slowed, then stopped.

"Everyone out!" a harsh voice shouted.

The voice came from the front of the tram. William could not make out who it was. The long trainful of miners rose slowly. Some climbed over the sides of cars; other waited for the small door and steps. William vaulted over the side and landed next to Dave. He reached up and helped Sandy down.

Dave was short, a few centimeters shorter than Sandy, and wore a big, bushy, black mustache. His curly black hair topped a rounded, cherubic face. The three of them lined up together.

"Let's go, let's go," someone at the front of the line said.

The line moved slowly; the miners were quiet. When William, Sandy, and Dave reached the head of the line, they saw a uniformed officer with an impatient, distracted look on his face. There were two men to his right and two to his left holding large, plastic cases. William caught sight of the foam lining and immediately knew what was expected. He approached one and turned around.

There was something different about this chip, William thought. The ones the company had inserted in him before had not bothered him. They had taken control of his motor functions smoothly. But this chip grated. It made him feel like he was grinding his teeth together, listening to someone scratch their nails over a piece of slate. He was totally unsettled.

The chip moved him jerkily, and his motions were unsteady. He was unprepared for the next direction the chip would deliver to his body. It pointed his head downward to watch for rubble on the stone path. As he walked, he watched his feet and arms move; but the movements were fluid, as natural as they had been with the other work chips.

There were probably breakdowns in the emotional and suppression circuits, William realized. Either that or these chips were not as refined as the others. He felt like he hadn't slept for days.

He found himself fighting. He wanted to stop to look for Sandy, to talk to some of the guards, but the more he fought, the worse he felt. He gave up and let the chip take over. Sleep was an alternative, but he doubted he could sleep feeling so unsettled, so uncomfortable. Besides, he was curious about where he was going and just what his new job would be.

He would wait.

William stood before a set of stainless steel rungs set into the tunnel wall. He wanted to look up, but the chip held firm control of his body. He climbed the rungs rapidly, easily. He counted them and, after the fifteenth, the chip made him swing himself off the ladder onto a platform. He was turned around so he faced a small tunnel: a conduit of metal. He was forced to his hands and knees and made to crawl into the tube.

The smell was overpowering.

The chip stopped him several meters inside. He reached up, groping in the dark for a bag hanging on a metal tab. He took it down and slung it over his back, totally confused. The smell got stronger. He felt himself gagging, but the chip suppressed his urge to vomit. He tasted bile.

An immobile black shape blocked his passage. Instead of having him crawl over it as he had expected, the chip made him stop. It was a small, amorphous blob and definitely the source of the smell. It was probably some kind of organic matter that had begun to decay.

The chip forced him to pick it up with his bare hands. Pieces of it detached and fell to the metal floor with a sickening thud. He stuffed its remains into the bag over his back.

It was repulsive and William retracted his mind, seeking retreat. He thought about Sandy and the new friend they had made, Dave. He could not understand what the control chip was demanding of him. The creature had begun to decompose. Was this his job? he wondered. Crawling through a conduit on his hands and knees, cleaning it of dead animals? Or was he simply doing some cleanup on his way?

He wished he had fallen asleep. When he got back to the barracks he would spend a lot of time in the shower stalls. Getting clean would take more than an antiseptic spray.

The last of the animal removed, he continued to crawl through the conduit. His progress was slow.

Some of the creatures were still alive, pulsating as they clung to the metal walls. When he pulled them off, they left a layer of sediment on the metal. And with that, he surmised that this was his job. If the company let these strange creatures thrive inside the conduits, they would soon clog it by their own presence or by their sedimentary wastes.

By the time he reached the end of the tunnel, the bag over his back was almost full. He pulled it off, glad to be free of the weight, and exited from the narrow chamber at the end of the conduit into another conduit. He retrieved another bag.

That was all he wanted to know.

Certain that this was his job, he was enraged. This was the kind of work more ably done by robot machinery. There was no need for him to be used in their stead. It was more than the degrading aspects of the job which annoyed him—the lack of logic in choosing human help over more efficient machines was ridiculous. And it felt like a punishment.

He consciously ignored the actions the control chip was making him do and concentrated on Sandy. He remembered what it was like before they had heard of the Morrison Mining Company, before he had lost his job. He remembered the short vacations and trips they had taken, and how nice it had been to return to their own safe, secure apartment.

It was good living then, he thought.

The chip was not programmed for a lunch break. By the end of the day, William's body smelled like the creatures he had removed from the conduits. He was exhausted, dirty, his knees scraped raw. Hands and arms were coated with the creatures' dried bodily fluids, caked, cracking everytime he moved.

He waited while the men in uniform walked up and down the ranks of miners callously yanking chips from their receptacles. William heard people fall to the ground. As he heard bootsteps approach, he braced himself; he would be faced with a tremendous rush of exhaustion as his body was returned to him.

There would be pain, too.

The bootsteps would stop, take two steps, stop, then continue. He could not turn his head to see, but he was sure he was next. He tensed every muscle he could in preparation to match the physical state the control chip had him in. That way, when the chip was yanked, his body would not be forced to make an immediate, massive adjustment. The closer his conscious mind was to the chip when it was removed, the smoother the takeover. Nothing. Another two steps. Nothing.

Then the chip was yanked out.

William felt every ache, every scrape, every pulled muscle in his body simultaneously. The pain centers in his brain had been suppressed. He relaxed slowly, section by section, afraid of letting himself go for fear of falling. He glanced up and down his row. At least half the miners were slumped on the ground. He felt his own control waver.

The smell, the dirt—it was too much.

But he held on. When the guards had finished, the same unarmed, uniformed officer walked up and faced the miners. He surveyed their crumpled ranks with a smirk, a hand resting on his hip.

He addressed them in a loud, clear voice. "You all now know what it's like to be a miner. You've only seen two sides. There are more. But there are ways to get back, ways to work yourselves up the ladder, but you must learn how." He looked at their faces. "Your precious indignation and outrage is comical. Take a good look at each other."

He turned and walked off.

"Back into the cars," a guard with a weapon ordered.

The miners did as they were told. They boarded the tram slowly, painfully, as if afraid to return to the barracks, and afraid to remain where they were.

They did little talking as the tram covered the length of track to the tunnel entrance. Before the cars reached the adit, a strong antiseptic-smelling liquid crashed down on them from above. William felt cleaner, and the powerful smell of the creatures was gone. The solution rained down for several minutes and he tilted his head back, luxuriating in the liquid bath. The solution stung his knees, elbows, and feet, but he put the pain aside. Getting clean seemed worth it.

Tired, beaten, the miners walked up the four cement steps and into Barracks 3. The older miners filed silently to their bunks and collapsed. The younger ones milled about, not wanting to join the group already in the showers, too tired to risk a short nap. The sitting area seemed to be the resting place, and William gravitated toward it. Besides, he told himself, the only way to the showers was through the sitting area.

He left Sandy and Dave talking, sitting on her bunk. There would be time for talking later; he did want to find out what jobs they had both performed, but the sitting area held what looked like the seeds of a meeting. If anything did develop out of it, there was a chance for him to help.

"Hey, Will," he heard a man's voice call from behind. William stopped and turned. Dave and Sandy were walking down the aisle between the triple-decker bunks. "Wait for us," Dave said.

When they caught up to him, Sandy asked, "What's going on back there?"

"I'm not sure. I was just going back to check it out."

"They look pretty nervous and upset," she commented.

William glanced at the miners over his shoulder and nodded in agreement. "Let's hear what they're saying."

They walked to the sitting area.

It was crowded, confusing; no one was in charge. Some miners around the fringe were standing, but most had found seats in chairs or on the cold floor. One man in his mid-thirties was talking, sitting with his long legs stretched out before him, crossed at the ankles.

The others around him listened, nodding their heads, interjecting a word or two of agreement until someone else interrupted with their own narration. Each person listened intently for a while, absorbed in the new person's life story until he, too, was interrupted and a new speaker took over.

William listened to three or four of them until he decided he had heard enough. Their stories had been similar. He tapped Sandy and Dave on their shoulders and motioned them back up the aisle. Once they were far enough away from the noise, William stopped.

"It's only a start, but I think there's something here," William said.

146

"What?" Dave asked.

"It's a nucleus," William answered. "They're all absorbed in their pasts right now—comparing notes, making sure where everyone stands, how much of their present situation was luck, how much pre-planned."

Sandy nodded. "When that person interrupted the guy who was first talking, there was hardly any break. It was like he was picking up threads of the first man's story."

"Yes," William said.

"But what happens when they run out of stories?" Dave asked.

"They'll realize they've run out of past and, hopefully, they'll turn their minds to the present."

"And then?" Sandy asked.

"And then we'll be right there—the three of us, pleading with them to do nothing. Not until we can get more information."

"Good," Dave said.

"I agree," Sandy said.

William hoped the others had the sense to see that acting now would be foolhardy. Any show of force, no matter how small, would be squashed by the guards. Now was the time for active waiting. Perhaps the hardest thing to do, he thought.

He remembered the surge of anger he had felt when he and Sandy had been sitting in their house just a few days ago. It seemed longer than that. He needed a quick outlet for his rage, but Sandy had convinced him to wait, to fight them on their own terms. Now he had to convince a group of depressed, upset miners to do the same thing: swallow their anger before their anger consumed them.

"There should be time to clean up," he told Sandy and Dave. "I'm going to take a shower while the meeting catches up to itself—or the present."

He was clean and he felt better. His knees did not bother him; most of the pain was gone and the skin over his kneecaps was stiff. It must have been the torrential downpour right before the mine exit, he thought. Some kind of antiseptic combined with nerve deadeners and something to speed up the healing process.

His stomach churned in hunger, but it would have to wait. It was early and there was still the meeting.

Sandy and Dave had rejoined the group and were listening to a young woman's story. William approached them and placed his hands on their shoulders. "How are they doing?" he asked softly.

"Pretty well," Sandy said. "They haven't reached what I would call a fevered pitch, but it has been consistently strong."

"Has any kind of leader appeared?"

"No. Are you thinking of stepping in and stoking the fire?" she asked.

He smiled. "No. I'm not going to do anything unless I have to."

"Stick around," Dave said. "You might have to."

William nodded. He stood in the back and waited for the explosion he was certain would happen. The discussion had picked up in tempo since he had last heard it, but whatever emotional outbursts there were, were short-lived. William was about to leave when Dave shouted at the man who was talking.

"So what! Who cares about your past!"

He elbowed his way through the crowd to the center of the sitting area.

"You're all reminiscing instead of planning. It's your futures that matter," Dave continued. A few hecklers started on him and were quickly warned off by those who wanted to listen. "You're weak—worse than children. Children don't have the experience you people do. Just like old men swapping stories about how glorious their youth was." He paced nervously, his short, compact body tracing a tight circle.

"There aren't that many guards in this detention camp," he said. "We can riot and free ourselves— make a break for it—"

"Wait a minute," William shouted over the yells and shouts of encouragement Dave had stirred. "Don't listen to this man. He and his ideas are only—"

"Shut up," Dave said. "I know these guards. Force is the only way to get anything done around here. They've been pushing us around for too long. They took my wife away from me and I tried talking— look what it got me! I haven't seen her since."

"I'm sorry about that," William said, "but you have to realize that force will only get you killed. What can you, or any one of us for that matter, accomplish if we're dead?"

"We can take some of them along with us," Dave said.

"Is that what you want to do? Become a martyr?" William asked. "You'll die senselessly."

"What do you know about all this?" Dave demanded.

"I know enough to think before I act. There are times to wait, and there are times to act."

"Then for God's sake, let's act!"

William shook his head. "That's insane. Listen with your mind—not your emotions. Here we are, several hundred tired, unarmed people, untrained in fighting, and you want us to stage an uprising— run outside and get cut to ribbons.

"It can't work. It won't work. We've got to take our time and plan things out," William said. "If you want to commit suicide, then run outside right now and try it. As for me, I'd much rather live. And if I can't live, then I'd like to die knowing my death did some good."

Dave stopped pacing and looked at William. "What kind of good are you talking about?" he asked. "If you're going to die, you might as well join the rest of us in the fighting. With everyone, we might stand a chance."

"No way, friend. Not me. What about all the others who landed on this hell-hole before us, and the ones who are probably landing right now? Do you think we're the first or last group of suckers to become miners for this company?"

"What?" Dave asked.

"We replaced the last group of miners who were in those houses just before us, just as another group is about to take our places. There are other barracks here, and other mining settlements on this planet."

"Yeah, I guess so. I never really thought about it."

"Then think, dammit. We'll only get one chance. Let's take it, use it, but let's take our time and think things out. Let's do it right."

"Okay," Dave said hesitantly. "I'll wait for now. For a while."

He extended his hand and William grasped it.

12

Morrison did not feel comfortable, and being comfortable was one of his primary avocations. He had eaten too much and his stomach bothered him. The hand-wrapped cigar protruding from his pouting lips was giving him a sore throat.

Bobbi was in her cabin. She had told him about her confrontation with Helene, and he did not want the two women to meet again. Helene had reacted badly, creating more pressure for him; Bobbi's youth and beauty had probably been too much for her to cope with. Dealing with her as an abstraction had never been difficult for Helene; Bobbi's flesh and blood appearance had probably given her that jolt.

Helene had looked tired. Morrison realized she was showing her age.

He motioned to the bartender, a man who looked put out every time he was asked for something. The man prepared the drink with cold, mechanical precision. He was a man Morrison could tolerate.

While sipping his drink, he decided to wait out Sherman. The spies, plants, and double agents would scurry around the surface of Lanta 2 until they found Sherman and brought him to the yacht. There was money involved—for anyone finding Sherman, Morrison would supply enough money to make them rich. And if no one found him soon enough, he would go back to the planet's surface himself and track him down.

He took a long pull from the glass and turned his mind to the domestic problems he faced on board.

Keeping Helene and Bobbi apart would not be easy. He could ask Bobbi not to leave her cabin and she would understand. She would be uncomfortable, nervous, pace the room like a caged tigress, but she would comply with his request. If necessary, he could lock her door from the outside, or post two guards outside in the passageway, alerted to the problem, he thought.

But dealing with Helene was another matter. He could not ask her to refrain from talking with Bobbi anymore. Even explaining that talking to her would only make her more unhappy might not work. If Helene had it in mind to confront Bobbi again, there would be no way he could stop her. A second meeting would only be an escalation of the first—they would not talk around the point as they had done, Morrison thought. If they met again, his life would be so disrupted there would be no living on the yacht with either of them.

Bobbi would be alienated from him; Helene could

accomplish that with incredible ease. Just like Sherman's ability to annoy, Morrison realized. In fact, they're both the same kind of person: singleminded, driven.

Andra walked into the lounge, lines of apprehension etched in her forehead. She walked steadily, legs always hidden under cloth: long pants, jumpsuits, dresses that reached her ankles. Morrison wondered what her legs looked like, why she always kept them hidden. Impulsively, he wanted to tell her to pull her long dress up to her waist, but he immediately ignored the urge. From the look on her face it was important.

"What is it, Andra?"

"Walters-Meyer."

"Yes?"

"He's lost Sherman," she said evenly.

Funny, he thought. She changes from day to day. There are times when she tries to cushion everything she tells me, and others when she just blurts it out. I wonder what makes the difference? he thought. "What happened? Give me some details."

"There are none. They never really picked up his trail after the plaza. The person they thought was him proved to be a dead end. Walters-Meyer says he's doing everything in his power to find him again. I told him to be prepared to meet your shuttle. It's ready, and the standby crew is waiting for you," she said.

"Tell them to go back to bed, or to go about doing whatever they were doing," he said, annoyed. "I'm not going anywhere. Not yet." He saw her eyebrows raise ever so slightly, then fall back to the noncommital mask of her face. "I want Lanta 2 to boil. Right now it's just warming up. My people aren't doing their jobs—not yet. We have to give them time."

153

She nodded and left the lounge.

He watched her legs as she walked, wondering if anything was wrong with them. He finished his drink.

"I'll have to consider it," the Sherman inside Alicia said, "but frankly, I don't think so."

"Put it to a vote," the Sherman inside Hanson said.

"No. No vote." He watched the shocked expression surface on the three faces. "There are still factors which may come to play later," he said in explanation. "Colonel Peterson is the head of the police force for this entire planet. He's not an easy man to approach. To involve him may not be beneficial."

The man harboring the red chip sat patiently listening.

"Vote," the Sherman in Hanson repeated.

"Yes," the Sherman in the cell member's body said. "I'd like a vote, too."

"And you?" he asked, addressing the red chip.

There was a lapse of a second or two, then the man spoke. "I would like to see this resolved, but voting is not the answer. None of us have the full picture. After all—there's the question of experiencing a situation—something only you have done. In this sense, your judgment is far superior to a vote."

Sherman nodded. "Then it's settled. You all know what to do." He rose to his feet and removed the chip from the cell member's body and told him to leave. The cell member with the red chip and Hanson remained. He withdrew the red chip and placed his hands on Alicia's hips, trying to present a powerful, intimidating figure in vain.

"How much do you remember?" the Sherman in Alicia asked.

154

"Enough."

"I don't think we can," the Sherman in Hanson said, answering the unasked question.

"Don't trust me," the man said. "If anything goes wrong, I don't want you looking for me."

"What makes you think we would?"

"The red chip. Your mind was clear to me—it told me. I understand what you're doing and I appreciate it. I'm thankful for it and don't want anything to go wrong. It's too important."

The Sherman in Alicia looked at the Sherman in Hanson for a decision. The Sherman in Hanson shrugged and turned away.

"All right, then. Get out," he said.

The man looked shocked and sat immobile.

"Didn't you hear me? I said get out. Or do you *want* to die?"

The man closed his mouth and was out the door in what seemed like a second. Sherman grinned as he watched the man's back disappear around the edge of the doorway.

"I knew you would let him go."

"Would you have?"

The Sherman in Hanson thought for a moment, then said, "Yes, I guess I would have."

The Sherman in Alicia sat down on the couch and crossed her legs. The jumpsuit was comfortable, but not something Alicia would have considered alluring. He pushed back her long, wavy hair and sighed.

"We should have used the man we just let go," the Sherman in Hanson said. "I could have transferred you from her body to his."

"I know what I did."

"Then why?"

"Sit down next to me and I'll show you."

The Sherman in Hanson walked the few steps to the couch and sat close to Alicia's body. Sherman slipped Alicia's arms around Hanson's neck so he felt taut breasts press into his side. There was little either of the Shermans could do to quell the surging emotions.

It had been a long time.

Four hands functioned as two, and each knew what the other wanted. There were no thoughts of hetero-, bi-, or homosexuality; for both of them, it was simply a matter of finally finding someone who understood—someone they could trust.

He took his time.

Later, after they had converted the living room to the bedroom furnishings, he rested in his arms. "Stay with me until we're ready," the Sherman in Alicia pleaded.

He looked at Alicia's face and smiled. "Are you sure it's a healthy situation?"

They laughed, and then he decided to stay until the plan would go into effect. Sherman was in no hurry—it was a good time to soothe the wounds his trail of destruction had caused inside him; it was a good time for learning more about himself, to get back some of the emotions and humanity he'd had to set aside.

And he had just the person to share this with.

Benjamin Douglas tried to think of the best way to explain why he had not taken his vacation. The company psychologist assigned to the Recruiting Division would be a hard person to convince. Selling a story to a psychologist was not the same as selling the homesteading idea to a young, eager, starving couple. If he had taken the mandatory week off, he would have lost the Maxwell-Rapps, the Cornva-Teutors, the Smythe-Johnsons, the Davis-

Frestones, the Allison-Brentnors, the Bellucis, the Kormoff-Perins, the ...

After dinner, William had the opportunity to talk to Dave. They took a walk outside the barracks before the sun set and the night air became frigid. William had asked Sandy to remain inside where she could keep track of any discussions in the sitting area. There weren't many people outside and William was almost at ease.

"I'm glad you did it," he said when they were alone.

"Sure. Don't worry about it," Dave said.

"Why did you start it?"

Dave looked at him and stopped walking, a bad thing to do; the ground was already cooling and his boots would not hold out the cold for long. "Someone had to do it. It didn't look like it was going anywhere. At least now it's in the open."

"You gave me a good fight."

"It had to look real."

"It did." William smiled at Dave; Dave did not return the smile. He stared at the ground, his mind somewhere else. "What is it, Dave? Your wife?"

"Partially," Dave said, eyes still looking downward. "I realize you don't really know anything about me—what I was doing before I signed up with this company. There's no way you could. Before I, well ... before Greta and I got into the company I wanted to be a meditech. I studied everything I could about human physiology, and was doing all right with my courses when money got tight. I never got to take much in the way of electronics. We tried to last it out, but we couldn't."

"And?" William said, unsure of what Dave was trying to say.

"I'm not sure, mind you, but I think we may be as good as dead no matter what we do."

William grabbed Dave's arm and pulled him into motion. "Let's keep moving." Once they had started off again, William asked him to explain further.

"It's the medulla."

"The what?"

"The medulla oblongata. Part of the hindbrain. It has absolute control over the body's respiration, digestion, and circulation. It controls breathing and blood pressure."

"What about it?" William asked.

"Do you know where it's located?"

"No. Not exactly."

"You'd better turn around." Dave spun William around, and Dave touched the back of his neck, directly above the spinal column. "Feel where I'm touching you?"

"No."

"That's because there's a piece of metal with a slot in it there."

William wheeled around. "What?"

Dave smiled weakly. "Whatever this mechanism is, however the receptacle works, it's located too close to the medulla for my satisfaction. The more the receptacle is used, the more the possible damage to the medulla."

"Are you sure about this?"

"No."

They started walking again, each locked into his own thoughts. They rounded a corner of the barracks and saw a young couple standing a few meters away, talking softly.

"How long would you say we have?" William asked.

"It's difficult to say. It would vary from person to

158

person, dependent on the receptacle's placement and the frequency of its use."

"The frequency of its use," William repeated.

They approached the front steps. A small group of children were sitting on the steps hurling insults at one another like they were playing with a rubber ball. When one made a particularly barbed comment they all roared with laughter.

"Let's not talk about this inside," William said. "There's no need to make matters worse."

"Worse? These people deserve to know the truth, the seriousness of their situation—"

"At which point they'll run outside and swarm the guards. You said yourself you're not certain about this," William said. "Let's give them time to organize first."

Dave shrugged. "You can tell them now, or tell them later—they'll still have to know."

"Let's go inside."

They walked up the steps and entered the building. The warmth was comforting; the level of noise was not. Children, too young to understand what all the shouting was about, cried in fear. Adults, too tired and on edge to keep their emotions under control, shouted at each other across bunks and aisles. William and Dave stood there, amazed and horrified. A few bunks down to their left, a woman lay on her bunk, wheezing, face flushed with fever.

The pandemonium continued. As they walked down the aisle looking for Sandy, William overheard several disagreements. He surmised that most of the shouting matches had started when someone who had overheard a family argument was foolish enough to offer a suggestion or comment. Other arguments consisted of territorial boundaries, infringement of privacy, property—it was insanity, he realized.

Sandy was on her bunk, hands clasped over her ears, eyes clamped shut. He glanced at the sitting area and a small group of young, muscular men were sitting, hunched over, heads close together in discussion.

"Sandy? Are you all right?" he asked, touching her shoulder.

She leaped up, surprised, then looked at him. She looked afraid and worried.

"Dave, will you see what's going on down there?" William asked.

"Sure."

When Dave had left, William stepped on his bunk and swung himself up next to Sandy. He held her close, tight, her head buried against his chest. He felt her body shake with sobs and he filled with anger. He wanted to climb up to the top bunk and shout everyone to silence, talk to them, redirect their anger and frustration away from each other and toward the guards. But the guards were not the answer, either. Maybe Dave was right—maybe they did need to know they were already dead.

He comforted Sandy as best he could. She had stopped sobbing and the noise around them had subsided a little. "I have to find out what's going on," William said softly.

"I'll go with you," she said.

"No. Stay here. Try to get some sleep."

"Sleep? That's cute, William. Sleep. I'll come with you," she said, following him to the floor.

He slipped an arm around her narrow waist and walked down the aisle to the sitting area. Dave had managed to become involved in their discussion and was dominating it. He stopped talking and looked up at William and Sandy as they approached.

"Still planning a suicidal rush for freedom?" William asked.

"No," Dave said, smiling. "Not at all."

One of the men looked William and Sandy up and down. "I don't know if you realize it or not," he said, "but what we're doing is against regulations. The rules are quite specific about this kind of meeting, and informing on those attending— maybe you'd be better off back at your bunks—"

"I know all about the rules," William said.

"Relax," Dave said. "These people are my friends. They're all our friends. There's no need to be defensive."

Dave handled the introductions and when he was finished, William and Sandy sat down with the group. "This is our core, then. Eight of us," William said.

Dave nodded.

"Have you told them about your medulla idea yet?"

"No. I was about to. Have you told Sandy?"

"Told me what?" Sandy asked.

He glanced at his wife. "No," he said, hoping the fear and worry on her face would not be increased by Dave's theory. "You may as well tell her at the same time."

"What?" Sandy asked.

"Listen to him and you'll find out," William said.

Dave explained his theory and William took that opportunity to give some consideration to potential informers. There were people who would be only too glad to sell out their fellow miners just to get out of the barracks. If all the miners understood about the medulla, then there was a chance they would band together to fight the man who had sentenced them to die. But there was also the chance they would react violently.

There was little he could do by himself, and eight people were not enough to form a decent organization. All it took was one person who could see that the easiest way out of the barracks was by informing.

Nonetheless, the miners deserved to know what Dave thought, he realized. Even if his theory was wrong, they deserved to hear it. There might even be another meditech in the group who could either confirm or deny Dave's theory.

"We've got to tell everyone," he said when Dave had finished. "You were right." He glanced at Sandy. The blood had drained from her face and she looked like she was ready to break. He squeezed her hand. "Come on," he told her. "Let's get some sleep."

She shook her head. "There'll be plenty of time to sleep later. Let's tell them now."

William heard the hard determination in her voice; it bordered on bitterness.

"All right. We'll tell them now."

Dave and the others in the group agreed.

"Where is he now?" Helene asked. She wore a formless dress that concealed her more than ample form. Morrison looked up at her.

"What?" he asked.

"I said I want to know where he is now."

"Do me a favor, Helene, will you?"

"What's that?"

"Leave me alone. This doesn't involve you."

"Doesn't involve me?" She leaned over, supporting her upper body by placing her hands on his chair arm. "It involves me as much as it involves you," she said, hate seething in her voice.

He wanted to smash her face with his hammy fist, throttle her until she gagged, choked, clawed at him for air. Or throw her out of the airlock without a suit . . . but then he wouldn't have the pleasure of hearing her scream as the oxygen fled her lungs in one tremendous rush.

The glass in his right hand cracked, then broke, falling to the deck in shards. Helene's face went white.

She always presses the wrong buttons, he thought.

"He is still on Lanta 2," he said, measuring his words. "The last time we had any direct contact with him was in a plaza, near the city of Alsis."

"Now," she demanded. "Tell me where he is *now!"*

He looked at her and smiled sardonically. "I don't care where he is now. I don't care what he's planning now. All the Donald Shermans in the Universe are down there," he said, pointing to the deck. "Sooner or later he'll make a mistake. He knows I'm here waiting, and he can't do anything by himself. He's got to have help—trust someone. Anyone. And as soon as he does that, I've got him."

"You're insane, Alexander. Do you know that?" she asked, backing away toward the door. "I never told you before, but you're insane."

Morrison sat in the oversized chair, amused and repelled by Helene's display. She ran from the lounge. He realized this gave him the opportunity to see Bobbi and spend some time with her. He pushed himself up from his chair and walked toward her cabin.

Maybe I should have dropped the chip and receptacle system, he thought as he walked through the passageways. That would have left Sherman virtually powerless. No, he still would have been able to use the escaped miners on the independents to do some damage. Changing the system would be too expensive, anyway—probably put me out of business.

Well, not out of business, he thought, but it would hurt.

He liked the idea of owning the people who worked for him.

And yet if he did not catch Sherman soon, irreparable damage would be done to his economic system. Chasing Sherman was still marginally more profitable than changing the chip and receptacle system, despite the discomfort involved.

It was obvious that Sherman was the insane one, out to take over the company. There was no other conceivable explanation for his actions—he had to be insane. Why, even if he succeeded in destroying me, Morrison thought, there's no way he could take over the company.

The door to Bobbi's cabin slid open and he entered to find her in front of a small holocube. She turned as she heard him enter.

"What are you watching?" he asked.

"James Joyce's *Ulysses*," she said.

"One of my favorites," he said. He stood behind her chair, one hand on the vinyl, the other on her shoulder.

"Did you ever stop and think about the way it was constructed? In its written form, it's really more Eastern than Western in thought," she said.

He smiled. "Never read it. I enjoy the dramatization too much, I guess. Reading it would only spoil the holo for me."

She shook her head and got up. "Why don't you sit down and tell me what's bothering you?" she asked. "I'll give you a little backrub while you tell me."

"What do you mean? There's nothing wrong."

"I can tell by your voice, Alex. Now sit down," she said, pulling him into the chair.

"I just need to spend some time with you. I'll take the backrub later. Maybe we should talk," he said hesitantly.

"Fine. What about?"

He did not answer. His mind was confused; thought after thought raced through his head like electrical relays clicking on and off; but none of the thoughts connected.

She lowered herself to the carpeted deck and put her hands on his knees. "Start at the beginning. We've known each other a long time and I've always asked you to leave him outside the door. Maybe I was wrong—I don't know. Start with Sherman."

He sighed from deep inside. "I don't even know why he's doing this to me. There are other mining companies, and yet none of them have the problems I have with Sherman.

"My people kept his early actions from me through some warped concept—they thought they were shielding me. They didn't want me upset. Upset!" He wiped his forehead with a silk handkerchief and leaned back in the chair. "Not only did that backfire, but it gave Sherman the time he needed to escape.

"He's never been in touch with me—never offered a list of demands for anything. I tell you I don't even know what he wants. I did get something that was supposed to be from him once, but it didn't make any sense. No sense whatsoever."

"What did it say?" Bobbi asked.

"I don't really remember. At the time he was just one of the thousand crackpots bothering me. Sherman isn't a crackpot, though. Those people who send you mail telling you they're going to kill you,

165

or kidnap you—they're harmless. It's the quiet ones you've got to watch out for. Look at Sherman. He's never said a word. Not one sound.

"Christ, I need a drink.

"If you'd seen the holograms of the cities and the communities he's wiped out. He uses some kind of gas on the people and they all die with contorted grins on their faces. The first time I saw what they looked like, I wanted to be sick. I wanted to kill him right there. I tried—"

"Alex?" Bobbi said.

"—to get as much information on him as I could, but it was only after, let's see, I can't remember... it was years later that I found out anything at all. Even then there was nothing concrete, nothing real about him. Sometimes I think—"

"Alex?" Bobbi said.

"—he isn't real at all, that he's only a figment of my imagination or something. Take Peterson for example. Peterson and Helene both think I'm out of my mind. And here's Peterson, head of a police network for a whole goddamned planet, and all he knows about Sherman is that he's a quasi-religious figure. When I told him I was here to find him, track him down, to wait him out if necessary, he looked at me like I was pursuing a phantom, like I was crazy. Maybe Peterson is right. Maybe Sherman doesn't exist at all."

He stopped and turned his head to face her, but she was gone. He looked around her cabin and saw her behind the bar, drinking. "Bobbi?"

"I'm glad you never told me this before, Alex. You make it sound like Sherman kills for pleasure."

"I don't know why he kills."

Bobbi crossed the room and handed Morrison a drink. "He must have a reason," she said. "No matter how warped, perverse, or twisted it is, he has a reason."

"I'm not so sure about that."

"And there's a reason why he chose you."

"Because I'm the biggest," he said weakly.

"That could be." She finished her drink and set the glass on the table.

"How about that backrub now?" Morrison asked.

"Sure," Bobbi said. "Why not?"

13

Sherman would have liked another week. The time spent with himself was doing him some good, but it was more important to move while everything was ready. All that remained were the two calls.

He thought of it as a vacation, a holiday in a locked room with himself. Alicia's body grew more comfortable and he appreciated it. So did the chip inside Hanson's body. They both delighted in her: one from the inside, one from the outside.

The Sherman in Hanson had started the week attempting to make up for lost time. He attacked everything with fresh, wondering eyes, like a child zealously following his mother through a shopping section in a plaza, stopping to peer through the stores' windows at toy displays. He commented on the food, the feel of the chairs, the way the floor felt underfoot. It was an adventure.

They planned when the holoset showed nothing of interest, or when either sex or eating was already done or soon to come. They went over and over the plan.

Contact had been made with Walters-Meyer, and Kenneth Hanson still had an important role to play. They were both wary of the chances involved.

Though the nights spent with Bobbi had been pleasant, restoring Morrison to a calmer, more stable state of mind, they had not made up for the torturous days.

A communications network had been established between his yacht and Walters-Meyer's office. Messages had been sent to Alsis, and when Walters-Meyer chose to respond, his answers were always vague. Morrison did not trust the man. He had failed to meet his commitment to Andra—Colonel Peterson had not been notified.

Then there was the fiasco in the plaza. Judging Walters-Meyer by Sewel-Tarkington's performance was impossible. Morrison had never met the man and knew nothing of his capabilities—he had only Walters-Meyer's word to go on.

And then there was the strange loyalty Walters-Meyer's men had for him. The only loyalty Morrison had been able to inspire was by making sure salaries were high.

After being on the yacht for three days with no solid information, no results from Alsis at all, he decided to send Andra to the planet's surface. If anyone could find out what was going on, she could.

Leaving it in her hands did not make him feel insecure. He was not apprehensive; she had done more difficult things for him in the past. But none, he felt, as important. With her in Alsis, he could sit back and wait for information to start coming in.

And it did.

He knew how Andra operated. She had moved into Walters-Meyer's house (probably his bedroom, too, Morrison thought) and gone everywhere he went. The fifth day after the plaza incident, Andra's second day with Walters-Meyer on Lanta 2, she had something on him.

She had linked him to the underground.

She radioed Morrison in code, in front of Walters-Meyer. Two days later she overheard a call from a woman who gave him the date, time, and location of a departing ship. Once Morrison had this information, he mustered whatever guards remained on the ship and boarded his shuttle with them.

Barracks 3 was quiet. A few object lessons had brought order to the lives of the miners.

William was exhausted. He lay next to Sandy, uncomfortable on the narrow bunk, determined to remain there despite the discomfort. Their relationship was disintegrating and talking about it was impossible; there were always too many ears.

"You going over to dinner?" Dave asked.

"I'll have to think about it," William said.

"What, about going over to dinner?" Dave asked incredulously.

"Wait a minute—what did I just say?"

"Forget it. You're tired. I'll see you later."

Dave walked to the door as if it were an effort.

Sandy shifted her position and William was forced to do the same so there would still be room. Relocation would occur after dinner, as it had once before, and the thought of it was distracting. Twenty miners transferred out, twenty miners transferred in, he thought. It was an unnerving ordeal—invariably, families were split up and new arrivals were nervous and disoriented for a while.

The guards were present through the entire process to ensure a smooth changeover. They had called off a list of twenty names and lined the miners up. The guard had then explained the process, the reasons for it, and that the names were chosen at random by computer.

The miners from the last relocation had been cautious at first, feeling out their new surroundings and companions. After the guards had left, William and Dave decided to proceed with their regular meeting as if nothing had happened. Once the new miners saw this, they approached William and Dave, asking to be included.

"The other barracks have similar organizations," one of the new men said.

"That's good to hear. At least the people who left will find it a little easier where they're going. I was afraid we were the only barracks that had organized," William said.

The man laughed. "We thought the same thing."

"Welcome, then. We're in this together."

The medulla theory had been corroborated by a woman in the barracks who had been trained as a meditech. William had explained the theory to the new arrivals and asked those miners leaving to spread the word. A few hours after the first relocation, the knowledge of the miners was equally shared.

And still there was no hope.

"Let's eat," Sandy said.

"All right," William said, though he was not hungry.

They climbed down from her bunk and walked to the Mess Hall.

171

The spaceport at Alsis was crowded. Morrison prayed that Andra's information had been correct; he could be in only one place, but Sherman was not held by these limitations. That fact alone caused his ulcer to burn with pain.

According to the information Andra had overheard, Sherman should be making his move anytime now, Morrison thought.

There were two shuttles, two transcontinental jets, and one f-t-l ship heading for another system, all leaving within five minutes of each other around the time Andra had told him.

Not many escaped miners could afford air travel, so the loading tubes to the ships did not require surveillance, Morrison reasoned. To be safe, he positioned a guard on the entrance tube leading to the f-t-l ship and the two transcontinental hops. The two shuttles, those unguarded, were bound for Lanta 1 and Lanta 3. He needed the rest of his men in the terminal lobby for detecting.

If Sherman went to either Lanta 1 or Lanta 3, Morrison would be in a much better position. He almost wished Sherman would slip through the tight net and board a shuttle for one of his planets. Then he would show Sherman how the game was played. On Lanta 2, Morrison knew he walked a thin line between being asked to leave and being arrested.

Walters-Meyer stood patiently by his side, scanning every entrance to the spaceport he could. Morrison knew what he was looking for and observed him closely. He was certain Walters-Meyer had no idea that he was aware of the link with Sherman via the underground. Unless, of course, Walters-Meyer had known all along and had arranged for Andra to overhear the wrong information.

But even if the information was false, Morrison

172

was still prepared—the other spaceports were conducting similar searches.

Four men circulated through the lobby in a different sector, each armed with a detector capable of locating any person who had a receptacle. Once they located someone, two men politely distracted the person while another man checked the back of his neck for a chip. Standard operating procedure, in effect since Morrison had first arrived at Lanta 2, necessary for locating Sherman.

If there was a chip, then he would have him.

The plan was simple, and he was sure it would work.

There's no way it can't, Morrison thought. Unless, of course, Sherman had trusted someone enough to transport the chips—but Sherman would not be that stupid. Anyone could sell Morrison the chips and live the rest of his life in luxury.

A group of ten people—eight men and two women —entered the terminal chatting amiably, looking around like tourists. Several were dressed in business suits; others wore sports clothes. One had a camera strapped around his neck. Morrison spotted the man almost immediately.

He was in his thirties, balding. The fringe around his scalp was brown, long, stringy, reaching below his shoulders. He was thin and pale with dark bags under his sunken eyes.

He looked distracted, eyes always moving, head turning in quick, jerky motions.

Morrison wasn't sure at first, but it looked strange enough to investigate. He glanced at Walters-Meyer; he was sweating. He told the man on his right to train his pistol on Walters-Meyer. "If he moves, shoot him," he instructed, then walked toward the group.

He kept his eyes steadily on the nervous man.

The man slowed, separating himself from the group by less than a meter. A man employed by Morrison was waving a detector around, accidentally got in Morrison's way, and was swept aside like an insect.

It was Sherman. Morrison was certain. It had to be him.

The man stopped while the nine others in his group continued through the lobby of the terminal. He glanced around nervously, turning his head first to his left, then to his right. Morrison judged the distance to the door behind the man. He could still get out—all he needed was a few more meters. Sherman hadn't spotted him, and was—

"That's him!" someone in the group of nine shouted, and was then hit over the head.

The man looked startled and wheeled around to flee, but it was too late. Morrison's men had surmised the situation and had leveled their pistols at him. Another band of Morrison's men surrounded the nine. Morrison moved forward purposely, breathing ragged, strangely unconscious of his weight. His eyes glazed over. He could already feel the man's windpipe collapse beneath his heavy thumbs, hear the neck snap, feel the chip crunch beneath his right foot.

As he strode forward, Morrison felt a tugging, a resistance on his arm, like a little dog who had sunk his teeth into a man's pants leg in an attempt to hold him back. He looked. It was Andra.

"Leave me alone," he said menacingly.

"Wait. We're not even sure it's Sherman," she said.

"It's him."

"How do you know? And what about local laws? Let's take him back to the yacht and be sure. We

174

can question him there—and you can do what you want to him in absolute safety."

Yes, he thought, there is time, now. My God, what was I thinking? There's no need to rush. I want to talk to him, explain what he's done to me, and find out *why* he did it. Find out what's behind all his insanity.

His men were holding the man. One of them held out a small gelatin capsule in his palm. "He tried to take this, sir," he said, showing it to Morrison.

Morrison thought of presenting it to Walters-Meyer as a parting gift—a reward for loyalty, but he was too elated. He instructed the man holding Walters-Meyer at gunpoint to let him go, then fired Walters-Meyer on the spot.

The normal flow of passengers had not been disrupted, and the terminal functioned normally. The activities of Morrison and his men did not affect them, and no one wanted to appear at a police investigation.

"Search him," Morrison instructed the guards. "Sherman, I'm surprised at you—and a little disappointed. I was hoping you'd run some more."

Sherman said nothing.

One of the guards pushed a blond man with drooping eyes toward Morrison with the muzzle of his gun. "This is the one who yelled."

"Name?" Morrison asked.

"Kenneth Hanson," he said, rubbing a large welt on his forehead.

"Why'd you do it?" Morrison asked.

Hanson motioned to Sherman. "He knows why, and that's all that counts. I wanted to kill him myself for what he did, but I have someone to go back to. You take the risks and take care of him."

Morrison looked puzzled and turned to Sherman.

"A woman," Sherman said.

"Alicia," Hanson said.

Morrison nodded. He withdrew a wad of bills from his pocket and presented them to Hanson.

"Keep your money," Hanson said. "I didn't do it for money."

Morrison shrugged, then instructed Andra to start clearing his men out. She let the group and Walters-Meyer leave. Sherman was alone with them.

"Nothing on him but this identity card," the man who had searched him said.

"Where are the rest of them?" Morrison asked Sherman.

Sherman shrugged. "Why not ask Colonel Peterson?" Morrison turned around, his hand straying to his right jacket pocket. "I'm sure he'd be glad to tell you."

"Any trouble?" Peterson asked.

"No," Morrison said, slipping his finger through the trigger guard of the small bore automatic in his pocket.

"I couldn't help but notice all your men here. Are you sure there's nothing wrong?"

"Yes. Quite sure. As you can see, my men are leaving and everything is under control." He kept the pistol leveled at Peterson's abdomen. "As a matter of fact, we were all just leaving."

Morrison did not know if Peterson suspected what was in his pocket, but he did not want to use the gun. However, if necessary, he would.

"And this man? Why is he being held?"

"A pickpocket. My men were lucky enough to detain him."

"Well, thanks for holding him until I arrived. I assume you'll want to press charges. We're rather strict with criminals here."

"No," Morrison said. "No harm done. Release

176

him," he ordered his men. He wasn't sure it was the right thing to do—he half expected Sherman to bolt for freedom. It would have been a shame to have to shoot him in the back, Morrison thought. Why didn't he run?

Sherman stood there, oddly calm. Peterson delivered a short lecture on interfering with police procedures and citizens' rights, then he and his four aides left.

Morrison, amazed, stared at Sherman. "Why didn't you tell him who you were? He would have taken you away, protected you. Why didn't you run?"

"I'm tired," Sherman said. "Besides—we've got a lot of memories to deal with yet."

Some guard had probably figured it out, William thought. Either that or the computer figured it out. Relocation seemed like a game to the company—someone must have reasoned that with full stomachs, the miners wouldn't mind being torn away from their families. So relocation took place after dinner. William tried very hard to look upon it as a game of chance; there was always the outside possibility of being sent back to your original barracks. Like playing Russian Roulette with only one empty chamber. A game played by a fool, a madman, or by someone who had no choice.

The guard walked in and read off twenty names. David Tanner-Snyder was the eighth name read. William clenched his fists. The company couldn't have broken the backbone of the organization any better if they had tried, he thought.

He was consoled by the thought that he and Sandy would remain together. At least until the next relocation.

Dave shrugged, grabbed his personal effects

177

from the locker beneath his bunk, and joined the others on line.

"That guard—does he look familiar?" William asked her. "I could have sworn I've seen him before."

"Yes, he does," she said thoughtfully. "Wasn't he one of the miners transferred out of here?"

"The one who slept over there," William said, pointing to a bunk near their own.

"I think it *is* him," Sandy said.

"From miner to guard," William said. "Well, that explains a hell of a lot."

"Like?"

"Like what the company does with miners who inform or do their 'Company Deeds,'" he said, quoting the list. "What better way to get enthusiastic guards, keen on performing their jobs? They're always afraid of slipping, falling back into the mines."

Sandy yawned and nodded her head.

The guard was staring back at them.

Another guard outside the barracks called for the twenty transfers. The miners left Barracks 3 quietly, knowing that struggling would only make it worse—less food, worse bunks, dirtier jobs; it wasn't worth it. The ones left behind tried to control themselves as friends, lovers, and family walked solemnly out the door.

The guard shifted his weight to the other foot and glanced quickly around the barracks, then returned his gaze to William and Sandy. He approached them.

He placed the rifle butt on the floor and leaned on it casually, hands on the muzzle to support his weight. "What's your name?" he asked in a cold tone.

William looked at the guard's piercing eyes, swallowed, then prepared to swing at him. Sandy's hand on his forearm stopped him in time. "William Carter," he answered bitterly.

"And you?"

"Sandy Carter."

"Thank you, Sandy Carter. You saved me from killing your husband."

"What—"

"Who's the leader of this barracks?" the guard asked.

"I don't know what you're talking about."

"I'll kill you if you don't tell me."

"And what happens if I do tell you?" William asked.

"You'll probably die."

William was confused. "And if I don't tell you?"

"You'll die right now."

A large group had gathered around. On William's word they could have swarmed over the guard and easily killed him. But the miners and William were curious, interested in finding out what the guard had in mind.

"He's the one," a young man shouted, pointing an accusing finger at William. "He's—"

The guard wheeled around and shot the young man, stopping his speech. He turned back to William and Sandy, smiling.

14

Morrison watched him constantly, afraid he might mysteriously vanish—ooze through the airlock, disappear through a porthole. He was afraid he might wake up at any moment to find himself in bed with Helene—first, the dream fantasy of capturing Sherman, then the nightmarish reality of being in bed with his wife. The shuttle was quiet.

With the initial joy of the capture subsided, anxiety crept in to replace elation. Morrison felt there was something wrong. He had chased Sherman too long to believe it could end so quickly, so easily.

"Where are the rest of them?" Morrison demanded. His voice echoed off the plain metal bulkheads.

Sherman continued to stare straight ahead.

"How many more chips are there?"

Nothing.

"You're going to talk to me, Sherman. You're going to tell me what I want to know."

Sherman turned his head and Morrison felt the man's glaring eyes. He quickly looked away. He had never seen such deep-rooted hatred before and was filled with a strange mixture of fear and elation. It wouldn't be long before the shuttle docked with his yacht—then he would have the opportunity to talk to Sherman in private. He realized it was a mistake to try to get him to talk now, with all the others around.

He sat quietly until the ship docked.

Sherman transferred before Morrison and once they were safely aboard the yacht, Sherman breathed a sigh of relief. Morrison was taken aback. He hustled Sherman into the lounge and cleared everyone out, including the ever-present silent bartender. He pointed to a chair and Sherman casually sauntered over to it.

Morrison paced back and forth before Sherman, aware he was not presenting a menacing impression, but unable to control himself. If he sat he would probably fidget, finger the pistol in his pocket.

"You don't even know who I am," Sherman said.

Morrison stopped his grotesque pacing. "I know. You're Donald Sherman."

Sherman laughed. "That's right." He laughed again, saw it was upsetting Morrison, then stopped. "What's the matter, Alex? Something bothering you? Something gnawing away at your insides?"

Morrison, determined not to let Sherman rile him, took a few deep breaths and settled into the chair across from him.

"It couldn't be all those miners you've killed, could it?"

Morrison looked aghast, then chuckled. "That's funny. All the miners I've killed." He exploded into raucous laughter. "That's a good one," he managed to say between gasps for air.

Sherman leaned forward and watched the fat man wheeze, waiting for him to catch his breath. "But it's true, Alex, you killed them. And many more like them."

Morrison could tell Sherman was serious. "Don't say that. Don't even imply it. It's not true, and it's not funny."

"It's not meant to be funny."

"Then what is it? An accusation?"

"No. Just a simple statement of fact. You've been killing miners since before I was born. I gave you the chance to right your mistakes. I gave you the benefit of the doubt."

"What are you talking about?" Morrison asked incredulously.

"I thought you could have been unaware of the situation. It seemed possible at the time—it wasn't beyond reason that a man so far removed from the everyday running of a company the size of yours could lose touch with the people—the miners who do the menial work."

"I don't understand."

"You could have been totally unaware of the miners altogether."

Morrison shook his head, annoyed. "What?"

"You do run a mining company, don't you?"

"You're insane."

"And you do have miners."

"Of course I have miners."

"And you know how they live."

"Sure."

"You see, Alex—"

"Don't call me that," Morrison interrupted.

Sherman pointed a slim, bony finger at Morrison. "I feel I should warn you, Alex—I'm not the last chip. If you plan to kill me, it would be a serious mistake."

"My men searched you. There are no other chips."

"I let myself be caught so I could talk to you. If you don't want to listen, I'll have to go on doing your killing for you. If you do listen, I'll call you whatever I like."

Morrison swallowed and stopped fondling the automatic through his jacket pocket—he hadn't realized he'd been doing it. "I could kill you now, Sherman. You say there are other chips. Maybe there are. But then again, maybe there aren't."

"Then kill me now and be done with it. Find out the hard way whether or not I'm telling you the truth. You've ignored everything I've asked of you, all the things I've brought to your attention. There's no reason to believe you'll listen to me now."

"You're not even making sense."

"I'm sure that's how you perceive it, my not making sense. But you're wrong. Perhaps I'm the only person you've ever talked to who does make sense."

Morrison shook his head and pushed himself out of the chair.

"Get me one, too," Sherman said.

Morrison continued toward the bar.

"You have any imicigs?"

"No," Morrison said, making a face. He finished fixing the drinks and walked back. He gave one to Sherman, then reached into an inner pocket and withdrew a hand-wrapped cigar. "Try one of these."

"Very civil of you."

Morrison grinned. "Not civil, Sherman. Everyone

should be treated to something special right before they die."

"Me? Die? You can't kill me." He prepared the cigar calmly, then lit it from Morrison's proffered lighter. "You can kill this body, crush this chip, but you'll never kill me."

Morrison gritted his teeth and leaned back in his chair. He had to determine whether or not Sherman was bluffing. If he was, and this was the last chip, then all he had to do was remove it and crush it. It would all end that simply. But if Sherman was not bluffing, Morrison realized he would have to proceed gingerly before taking any definitive action.

The door to the lounge slid open and Helene walked in.

"Get out," Morrison said.

"Is that him?" she asked, ignoring Morrison's demand. "Are you Donald Sherman?"

"I said get out!"

"Yes, I'm Sherman. Who are you?"

Helene stood awkwardly, paused in mid-stride, unsure if she should come closer or if she were close enough.

"Helene, will you get out? I'm sorry, Sherman. My wife is not well."

Sherman smiled weakly; Morrison assumed it was his attempt at an understanding expression.

"Where is he?" Helene demanded.

"Ignore her, Sherman." Morrison rose and approached his wife.

"Where *is* he?" she demanded again.

Sherman turned toward her. "Who?" he asked.

Morrison grabbed her and shook her by the shoulders. "Will you leave us alone?"

"Who?" Sherman repeated.

Helene was crying.

"Leave her alone, Morrison."

Morrison dropped his grip on Helene and spun around. "Stay out of this—it doesn't concern you."

"Doesn't concern him?" shrieked Helene.

"What's this all about?"

"Tell me please. Where is he, Sherman?" she pleaded hysterically.

"Who, dammit? You've got to tell me who you're talking about."

"Vladimir," she managed to say through her sobbing.

"Vladimir?" Sherman said.

Morrison looked like he had been run over and dragged a hundred meters. He hung his head and walked slowly back to his chair. He collapsed into it.

"Vladimir Leaw-Zabinski?" Sherman asked.

She nodded.

"How do you know Vladimir?" he asked.

"He was my husband . . . once. Where is he now?"

Sherman could not believe it. Even as a young man, listening to Vladimir's stories about Morrison and his wife, he thought they were exaggerations. "You never told her," Sherman said to Morrison. "All this time, and you never told her."

Helene stared wild-eyed at her husband as he slowly shook his head. "You don't understand, Sherman—I didn't know. It wasn't my doing."

"Right," Sherman said disdainfully. "It never is, is it?"

Helene's eyes were glazed, unblinking, tears streaming down her cheeks.

"Some overzealous employee thought it was the right thing to do. I fired him immediately."

"You killed him," Helene said softly. "You killed Vladimir."

"Helene," he pleaded.

"You bastard. You lousy goddamned bastard."

She turned and strode out of the lounge. The two men sat in heavy silence. Morrison, hands on his forehead, shading his eyes, stared at the deck. Sherman smoked his cigar and sipped his drink patiently.

"You've been nothing but trouble for me, Sherman."

"As long as you continue to treat people like you do, I'll continue to be trouble."

"Back to the miners again," Morrison said, sighing.

"What about your wife? Is she a miner, too?"

Morrison took a long pull from his drink. "What is it you want of me?"

"One thing at a time. Is she or isn't she a miner?"

"No, Sherman. She is not a miner," he said, tired. "Now tell me what you want."

"I'm not so sure. At first I wanted to kill you. Then I realized that killing you wouldn't solve anything. I sent you the communication outlining the changes I wanted to see in your mining system. The recommendations could have changed your company from a vile, sadistic, inhuman organization to one which takes care of the people working for it.

"After waiting months, what I considered a fair length of time for your answer, I did what I had to do. Now, I'm tired.

"I had hoped to stir some feelings in your corpulent carcass—some feelings of humanity—but I realize I've failed at that. You're now harder, crueler —a man who cares about nothing but himself and his money," Sherman said calmly.

"You really *are* insane," Morrison said.

"Perhaps I am," Sherman said. "Perhaps I am.

Because of this, though, the destruction will continue."

"Because of what?"

"Your lack of cooperation, my insanity, your unchanging attitude, your—"

"Enough!" Morrison shouted. "I have heard quite enough. There's no reason to continue at this time."

"Oh, have you really had enough?" Sherman asked sarcastically.

"That's all, Sherman. I'm going to get some sleep. Despite your attitude, I'm willing to give you a choice: remain inside your body and make no trouble, or be removed now."

"I'll stay in the body. Don't worry, Alex. I don't have to make trouble—the other chips are busily at work."

"There will be four guards—two inside your cabin, two outside in the passageway. These men will not hesitate to kill the body you're in. We have others aboard who have receptacles."

Morrison rose and walked to the door. He told four guards stationed outside the lounge to escort Sherman to one of the spare cabins and gave them detailed instructions, including the penalty for failure. When he was certain they all understood, he waited until they had escorted Sherman down the passageway and around a corner, out of sight.

Morrison needed a shower and a change of clothes; he hadn't realized how much he had sweated. His clothes made him feel clammy.

As the door opened he saw Helene at her vanity, staring blankly at her own reflection. He did not stop to talk with her, deciding it was better to let her work her way out of shock and grief by herself.

187

He had let a whole group of men and women do that in the past and they had repaid his thoughtfulness by building him a mining company.

There was no possible way he could have gotten to where he was without their help, he realized.

The War had been long, hard, brutal, drawn out by both sides to help level off the population. As in every war, there were economic and territorial factors involved, Morrison thought as he stripped away his damp clothes. And like every war, there were prisoners. It seemed like it had happened in a different life—he recalled it only as a brief memory.

The camps the enemy had set up were impressive only in their spartan brutality. Escape would not have been a real problem for anyone who attempted it. Camp leaders did not like the idea of funneling food from their own people in uniform to the prisoners. So they made it easy for anyone who wished to escape.

Morrison, young, eager, athletic, had been caught in an ambush and taken prisoner. It was hard for him to remember what he looked like or felt then. That was where he had met Vladimir.

He stepped into the shower and was sprayed with a fine mist of pure water. The use of water was a luxury he revelled in.

The only difficulty in effecting the escape, he remembered, had been in talking his fellow prisoners into going along. They were in no rush to relinquish their safe positions for the danger of their own front lines. Many liked the prison camp's food more than the food they had eaten before capture. Even with Vladimir's help, it took months of slow, cautious persuasion before he had a small group of men and women.

The actual escape was uneventful, the details

forgotten. It was what came soon after that Morrison liked to remember best.

After the War had ended, his fellow escapees and ex-prisoners were grateful for his help. Many returned home to find they no longer had families, jobs, or homes. Morrison had started an import-export business once trade had been reestablished, and these people had come to him for jobs. He helped them out once again and, with their help, the small import-export business mushroomed into the Morrison Mining Company.

He dried himself and, suddenly aware of someone else's presence in the bathroom, spun around. It was Helene. He didn't know what to say to her—with her knowing about what had happened to Vladimir, there was no telling what she was thinking.

"What is it, Helene?" he asked softly.

"I was just thinking—you could stand to lose some weight."

Her statement hit him hard. Naked, a towel held up before his obese form, he tried to deal with the implications of her statement.

"Yes," he said hesitantly, "I guess I could."

"When are we going back, Alex?" she asked.

It was difficult for him to keep control. She hadn't called him Alex in years. "Soon, Helene. We'll go soon."

"Good." She turned and left him alone.

He stood in stunned silence, then resumed his toweling. The shock of finding out her ex-husband was dead must have done something to her, Morrison realized. The fire was gone; all the hatred and venom she had directed at him was dissolved and, though she was not endearing, she was being pleasant.

He felt strangely unsettled. He wanted to talk to

her, find out what she was thinking, how she had taken the shock, and maybe even ask her advice on Sherman. It wouldn't be difficult to walk out there and just sit down and talk, he reasoned. But he hesitated. There were still too many years fending barbed comments and insults to let it all slide because of a few minutes.

He tied the sash on his robe. He would talk to Bobbi first, find out what she thought of the situation with Sherman. Then, if Helene's mood held, he would talk to her.

She shook her head slowly in disbelief. "I want to talk to him," Bobbi said.

Morrison shrugged. "Why?"

"You want my advice? I'm not giving you any until I talk to him myself." She stepped into the translucent jumpsuit. "This isn't a question of buying, selling, expanding—it's something else entirely. You know that. I can't go by only your opinions this time."

"All right. Talk to him. Five minutes."

"Alex," she said sternly.

"All right, all right. But change your clothes."

"What?"

"You want to see him, but there's no need for him to see all of you."

Benjamin Douglas watched the market plunge, then soar, then fluctuate in near stability. It made him a happy man; an unstable market meant more people out of work and less jobs for those already jobless.

His landlord had tried to raise the rent on his apartment. It was a small room without major appliances or conveniences. Although he could have easily afforded the increase, he sued the landlord for not supplying adequate services. Douglas had shown up for the small-claims trial; the landlord had not. Douglas had won the case.

That month, Douglas won the Sales Division's bonus and raised the Recruitment Division's average by .01 percent. It was something he was proud of.

He decided that on retiring, he would take some of his savings and use them for a trip, maybe to Randu to see where all those happy, young couples he had recruited ended up. Maybe, he thought, if I like it enough, I just might stay there for a while.

She was in no rush to return to her cabin, but she could not remain in the passageway for long. Alex was probably pacing, trying to decide whether or not to burst through the door to Sherman's cabin. She stayed longer than she had expected, and now she had to go back and face Morrison, she realized, chewing on a fingernail.

Bobbi took a deep breath and pressed on to her cabin. She hoped he hadn't started drinking.

She turned the corner two doors away from her cabin to see Helene leaning against the bulkhead, waiting. She was startled and about to say something when Helene lunged at her. Bobbi tried backing away, but Helene's larger form, already in motion, overtook her, throwing her to the deck.

Helene's open fists smashed into her, nails raking, gouging, as Bobbi tried to protect her eyes. The woman's larger, heavier body kept Bobbi pinned to the deck.

She screamed.

The noise was cut off as Helene slipped her trembling hands around Bobbi's throat, cutting off her air. All Bobbi could see was the maniacal expression on Helene's face. Blood pounded in her ears and she struggled, trying to kick, smash, bite Helene someplace.

And then the weight was gone, the air rushed back into her lungs as she gasped for breath. She looked up to see Helene held high in the air, then thrown hard against the bulkhead. Her body hit then landed with a sickening thud and a snap. Then she saw Morrison.

His face was flushed, his eyes wide open, his hands trembling. Bobbi looked at Helene, her arms and legs twisted in impossible positions. Her eyes were open, glassy.

Bobbi pushed herself up and stood shakily. She tottered over to Helene and felt for a pulse.

There was none.

Morrison was seated in the huge chair he liked to use, watching the holotape play in an endless loop, the sound turned down on the modernization of *Macbeth*. "Well?" he asked, still facing the miniature players.

"She's not even frozen yet, Alex. I don't want to talk."

He turned to her, eyebrows raised. "Oh? In fact, Helene's remains are locked in the deep-freeze. She was frozen almost instantly. Now sit down and tell me."

Bobbi forced another mouthful of liquor down and tried to stop shaking. "She wasn't going to kill me, Alex. She was too weak. She couldn't have killed me. I was just too shocked to do anything else to stop her. She was—"

"I know. Crazy. We've been through the whole thing now three times. I told you I was sorry, that I didn't mean to kill her. I didn't realize what I was doing. I didn't think. Now sit down and tell me."

192

She moved around his chair and stood in front of the holocube. "It's not that easy. Not anymore." She took another sip. "Why did she do it, Alex?"

"Sherman," he said firmly. "Tell me what you think about Sherman. Then we'll talk about her."

"Tell me why she did it. I don't understand. I never did anything to hurt her—"

"Hate," he said. "She did it because she hated me. She always hated me—for Vladimir, I suppose—and this was the only way she figured she could get to me."

She fixed herself another drink, then walked back to his chair. "You think she hated you that much?"

"Yes."

"I never saw you like that, Alex ... seething with rage. All you had to do was pick her up and put her down. But you killed her."

"I know that," he said through clenched teeth. "And I'm sorry I did, but we don't have much time left. Sherman is waiting for an answer. He has to know. I have to know."

She put down her drink and rubbed her eyes. "All right. You tell me—what do you plan to do?"

"I'm not sure." He leaned forward, his eyebrows almost meeting. "I've been chasing him for years and I still don't know a goddamn thing about him except he's insane. There's no way for me to judge if he's bluffing if I don't know him."

"And if you think he *is* bluffing? What then?"

"Then I've got him right where I want him," he said, his gray eyes sparkling. It reminded her of how he looked after Helene landed on the deck. She stifled a shudder.

"Yes, but what will you do?" she asked.

"Do? I'll remove the chip and save it. Yes. I'll save it—have it made into a belt buckle. If I'd saved the first one I could have made them into cuff links."

"Is that supposed to be funny?" she demanded.

He sighed. "I'll keep the chip. I'll reinsert it once a year and tell him what he's been missing. Or let him do whatever he wants for that day. He would have to be guarded..."

"That would be torture," Bobbi said.

"As Sherman says, perhaps."

She had heard enough. After the doubts, suspicions, and fears Sherman had stirred in her, and after seeing what he had done to Helene, she realized Morrison was not the man she thought she knew. "All right then, Alex. I'm ready to talk to you about this—this situation you've gotten yourself into."

"Me?"

"I'm going to recount to you what happened and, when I'm done, I'd appreciate your leaving me alone for a while."

Bobbi told him about Sherman's background, ignoring his protests and interruptions. She explained how he had used Morrison's men to flee Sanbar 5, the planet on which Sherman had met Vladimir. The parts that Morrison had already heard or had known about before caused him to fidget. But Bobbi continued, explaining what was in the original communication he had sent to Morrison.

"Drop the chip and receptacle system?" he asked, outraged.

"Or at least relocate the receptacle and its mechanisms. Remember what happened to his parents," Bobbi said.

Morrison nodded once. "What else?"

"Change the living conditions for the miners."

"They're treated well enough."

"Do you understand what living like that can do to a family with children? Or even a married couple? Have you any idea how cruel that barracks system

194

is? The miners aren't being treated as well as cattle. I knew it was bad, Alex, but I never thought it was like this."

"Aren't you being a bit naive?" he asked. "Any business this size doesn't come into being and stay this big without a few distasteful situations."

"But Alex—there are limits. And that's what I'm talking about. Limits. I've reached mine with you. For now. Sherman explained how it really is. He made me see—"

"So you believe him and not me, huh?"

"No, it isn't that. Even if I compromised what he said, how he sees it, and the way you see it, it would still be intolerable.

"Kill him, torture him, or even consider calling his bluff and you're worse than he is," Bobbi said.

"What?"

"You heard me. Worse. You put on a pretty good show of being horrified by mass murder, by the deaths of your own miners. But instead of ending Sherman's atrocities by changing your system, by losing a little money, you let it go on by chasing a madman across the galaxy."

She saw he was about to interrupt and cut him off with a wave of her hand. "You're the one who's been doing all the killing. You're the one—all those miners, slowly, each and every one of them by using this chip and receptacle system. I have never particularly enjoyed talking business with you, and in all the time I've known you, I've taken your side. Until I saw what you did to Helene, I wasn't sure.

"Please Alex—show me whether I was right or wrong. Go into his room and talk to him, listen to him, find out what he wants you to do."

Morrison said nothing.

"If you don't," Bobbi said, "you can find yourself a new mistress."

15

The miners stood in shocked silence. Those near the body moved away from the bloody remains. None of the others reacted at all. Attack the guard? But he had actually done them a service by weeding out an informer. Nonetheless, they were not grateful.

William looked long and hard at the guard. There was something different about him—something in his face was stronger, harder than as he remembered him. Perhaps that's what being a guard does to you, he thought.

"Was that necessary?" William asked.

"I think it was. If not now, then later," the guard

said. "I've traveled too far to be stopped by some scared, little, loud-mouthed miner."

The miners tensed, waiting for William to say something, do something. "What do you mean, too far?"

"Have two men take care of the body now. When they come back I'll explain everything to all of you."

William did as the guard requested and waited impatiently for his men's return. The guard suggested they wait in the sitting area and the miners moved down to the end of the barracks. Children, quiet with fear, followed. By the time the miners had settled themselves, the two men returned.

The guard addressed them.

"My name is Donald Sherman," the guard said. Some miners mumbled words of recognition. "I was a miner once. It was a different planet, a different solar system and the rules and regulations were a little different, but I was still a miner.

"My parents were murdered by Morrison, just as he's slowly murdering each and every one of you." He paused to look over the group. "The receptacle implanted in the back of your necks will eventually cause irreparable damage to a portion of your brains, the medulla—"

"We know all about the medulla," William interrupted.

Sherman looked surprised for a moment, then continued. "I've been trying to get Morrison to change his system for years. In barracks worse than this, people have begged me, pleaded with me to put them out of their miserable existence by helping them revolt. They knew they would lose, but they thought it would help change things.

"I helped in the past—perhaps too many times. I've killed many people, destroyed much of Morrison's equipment. Now I'm coming to you to help me put an end to the destruction. I need your help."

"What kind of help?" Sandy asked.

"On board Morrison's yacht right now, there's a body with a chip of mine inside it. If all went well, then he's explained what has happened and is arranging a meeting between Morrison and one of you."

"So you can kill him?" William asked.

"What I have to do to solve this problem we're trapped in is my affair."

"Not if I decide to help," William said.

"If you want to help, then you'll know. I'll tell you when the time comes."

"Go on," William said.

"No," Sandy said. "Tell us how you got here."

"I could show you the whole thing, share my entire life with you in less than a second." Sherman reached into his uniform and withdrew a small, plastic case. He snapped it open. "I exist only as a chip. My entire personality has been recorded on these white control chips. This red one cannot control the person it's inserted into, but the person does share my mind."

William stared at him as if he were crazy.

"I had to sacrifice one of these white chips at a spaceport at Alsis, on Lanta 2. That's the chip with Morrison now. While Morrison was occupied with the capture, I slipped through and boarded the shuttle for this planet. Once the shuttle landed, I inserted my spare chip into an employee, removed the other, sent the original body back to—does this really matter?" Sherman asked.

"Not if you can prove what you say," William said.

"I can." He removed a white chip. "Pick anyone here."

William suggested himself.

Sherman inserted the chip into William's neck. That convinced the miners and he withdrew the chip.

"What happened?" William asked.

"Nothing exceptional," Sandy said. "But you did say something you wouldn't have ordinarily said."

"What?" William asked.

"You said your name was Donald Sherman."

"All right. What do we have to do, Sherman?" William asked.

Morrison talked to the head of security right before he entered the shuttle. Even after the man had prepared him, Morrison still felt naked. Taking his shuttle to the prearranged spot with Sherman left behind on the yacht, and a Sherman loose on Lanta 3, made him think he was the crazy one—not Sherman.

He knew what he was supposed to do.

He knew what was expected of him.

Sherman had been extremely lucid explaining what he had to do to call an end to the killing and the destruction. Sherman had watched and listened as Morrison slowly, but efficiently, altered his mining company. The meditechs had been called and ordered to redesign and relocate the receptacle on all miners. The security officers on each of his planets were notified by the head of security on Morrison's yacht.

Well, reflected Morrison, at least I won't have to pay off the Interplanetary Monitors anymore and there's something positive to that. They won't be able to bleed me any longer for violating their indentured employee clause.

Sherman had waited almost forty-eight hours before telling Morrison to proceed. Sherman had probably wanted to make sure the changes wouldn't be countermanded as soon as he had left for Lanta 3.

At last he told Morrison where the rendezvous was to be. He also told him to go alone. If the Sherman on Lanta 3 saw that he was not alone, he had instructions to continue the destruction. He handed Morrison a coded note and wished him luck with a smirk on his face.

Morrison had then gone directly to his chief of security and explained that he needed quick, lethal, concealed weapons. But even loaded down with weapons, Morrison felt naked.

Inside the metal skin of the shuttle was only one other person: the captain. It was the first time Morrison could remember being alone since the War.

He wished he was back in bed with Bobbi.

The news spread quickly from barracks to barracks. At exactly the same moment, miners swarmed out of their buildings and, led by Sherman, took over the small camp. There had been little resistance. They settled in to wait for Morrison's shuttle.

Sherman turned William around and placed the red chip in the back of his neck. William, in a rush, knew all there was to know about Donald Sherman.

It filled him with loathing and rage when he realized just what Morrison had done to so many people, and what Sherman had done to an almost equal number.

He turned and saw Sandy as if for the first time in many months. She looked halfstarved, and creases, like rays, spread out from the corners of her eyes. Her shoulders slumped forward, her skin chalky white—

"Are you ready?" Sherman asked.

Remove the chip from the guard's slot and put it in the case.

"I'm ready," William said, reluctantly doing as the red chip instructed. It was not an easy thing for him to reconcile, being used as a marionette, taking—

Let's go. That's his ship settling down.

William watched the dust the ship raised as it settled down a hundred meters away from the encampment. He took one last look at Sandy, *Let's go*, kissed her good-bye, *Carter, let's go!* and set off to meet Morrison's ship.

Morrison's ship, William thought. And inside it is a man who would just as soon kill me as say hello, a man whose values are so clearly defined, so blatantly obvious, that Sherman needed me as a sacrifice before the slaughter. It's suicide.

He stopped walking and turned back to look at the camp. He felt the expectant eyes on him, the hopes of the miners and of Sandy, and knew then he could not turn back.

He turned and walked on, thinking of how he might have to kill Morrison in self-defense, then immediately realized his mistake.

Don't. Kill him and everything I've worked for is gone.

Right, William thought, pressing on through the ugly terrain. Anything you say.

The door to the shuttle opened to reveal a grossly obese man.

That's him.

I'm going to do it, Sherman. I'm going to kill him for what he did to Sandy, William thought.

Don't! You don't understand!

William ignored the red chip's pleading and fondled the small, plastic case in his pocket. He snapped it open and felt the chips. Inside the case were two white chips. He knew from the red chip that Morrison had the last white chip in custody.

Despite the chilling breeze, sweat began to bead on William's forehead. Morrison had climbed down the ladder and was approaching on foot.

Good. He's going to do it.

And I'm going to kill him, William thought.

I won't let you!

You can't stop me. I'll have to kill him—he's going to kill me. It's easy for you—dead, existing only as a chip. You don't have a wife waiting for you. You don't have friends waiting for you. What the hell do you know besides killing? Good-by, Sherman, William thought as he reached back to his neck and touched the chip to—

Wait!

Ten meters separated William from Morrison.

At least let me find out if he's agreed.

William dropped his hand to his side, continued walking, then stopped before Morrison. Morrison placed a folded piece of paper into William's hand. William waited for the paper to explode, for the acid to eat its way through his hand and up his arm, for the contact poison to be asborbed through his finger tips, but nothing happened. Before he opened the paper, he looked at Morrison's eyes. Morrison's face was a mask of total fear.

Open it.

William unfolded the note. It was a series of numbers, and through the red chip, he understood what it meant.

He's agreed. The first steps have already been taken.

William smiled and reached up to the back of his neck.

Wait! Don't kill—

He placed the withdrawn red chip into the small, plastic case beside the remaining white one. He hoped Sherman hadn't told Morrison how many chips there were, that Morrison didn't notice. He handed him the case.

Morrison smiled.

William took a deep breath and turned his back on the man, starting to walk straight for the barracks, for Sandy. He waited while he walked, expecting the bullet between the shoulder blades, the laser slicing throught his back, cauterizing the wound on its way through, but nothing happened. Nothing.

He couldn't believe it. He started breathing again.

He refused to look back at Morrison.

He patted the top pocket of his thermalsuit. Inside of it rested a small, white chip of plastic.

Just in case, William thought. Just in case.

The docking procedure seemed to take forever. Morrison held the small, plastic case in his lap, afraid to make any sudden movements for fear of setting off one of the delicate weapons concealed on his body. Every time the shuttle bumped against his yacht, Morrison winced.

He waited for the door to cycle open, holding the chips tightly in his hand. The weapons hadn't been needed, and he considered going straight to security to have them removed from his body. Sherman could wait.

He wanted to show Sherman the case and tell him it was over; that now, with the chips, there would be no reason to go through with the rest of the changes Sherman had demanded.

He would have to handle the situation carefully.

The door slid open slowly and he walked onto the yacht. Bobbi was waiting for him in the passageway, smiling, eyebrows raised in hopeful anticipation.

"Where is he?" Morrison asked.

"Still in his cabin."

"Do me a favor, will you? Tell him I want to see him in the lounge."

"Did it go all right?" Bobbi asked.

He smiled. "Of course. I wasn't planning on taking any chances."

"Well, if everything went so well, it would be a lot better if you went to see him."

"Yes, I guess it would." His smile faded and his eyes hardened. "Tell him I want to see him."

Bobbi stared at him for a long moment, then nodded. "All right. I'll tell him."

Morrison watched her move down the passageway toward Sherman's cabin. She moved gracefully, but he could see that she was tense—too tense. Something about her had changed. Things were different now that Helene was in the deep-freeze. Bobbi seemed to be taking Helene's place, giving him orders, telling him the right thing to do and how he should do it. It wasn't right. One Helene was more than enough.

He went to the head of security to have the weapons removed.

The miners were outside, milling around, talking to each other and to the guards. There were no rifles being pointed, no orders being given.

William sat on his bunk, shaking. He felt totally empty, washed out, tired. He couldn't control his hands—they trembled when he held them out straight. He was glad none of the other miners were inside the building to see him. Sandy sat beside him, smiling softly, tenderly, holding his hands in hers.

"You did it, William. It's okay, now," she said.

He glared at her, hurt, angry, and frustrated. "I wanted to kill him."

She squeezed his hands. "I know. But you didn't. And that's what counts."

He wheeled around, fists clenched. "Is it? Is it really? He got away. He strolled back to his shuttle and flew off. He left us here. All of us."

She nodded. "That's true. He did. But things are going to be different from now on. Sherman promised us."

"Sure he promised. But what makes you think he's any better? What makes you think he's going to make any difference in the long run?"

"He will. You'll see."

He shook his head. "Sure."

Sandy slipped an arm around his shoulder. "Take it easy, Will. You're still worked up. You don't know what you're saying."

"I know what I'm saying, all right. I wanted to kill him. And I would have, too, if it hadn't been for that damned red chip of his. He distracted me, kept me busy until it was too late. I wanted to kill him for you, baby."

She moved away suddenly, looking at him as if he'd just told her he didn't love her anymore. "For me? Why?"

"For what he did to us."

"What did he do? What could he do to us? We're still together, aren't we? Isn't that what matters? Or don't you believe what you've been telling me?"

He looked at her, saw that she meant it, then threw his arms around her. They hugged, crying for each other.

Morrison was stripped of all the automatic weapons, sitting in his chair near the middle of the lounge. He sipped his drink idly, waiting for Bobbi and Sherman. They should have been here already, prepared to listen to how it was going to be from now on.

Helene was dead. Perhaps it would be best if she stayed that way, he thought.

He shrugged and took another sip of his drink.

It was all working out perfectly. Sherman had believed him, had believed the changes would be permanent, but that was *his* problem. It had gotten Morrison the chips, and that was all that counted. As long as there weren't any more of them floating around. He would have to be sure of that before saying anything to either of them about his plans. And if Sherman gave him any trouble, there was always the automatic in his jacket pocket.

They walked in together, like two conspirators, making Morrison immediately suspicious. They looked like they'd been talking about something— something they didn't want Morrison to know. Bobbi was looking at him funny, in that same way she had when she'd delivered her ultimatum.

Sherman smiled and sat across from Morrison.

"I see you got the case," Sherman said.

Morrison held it up. "How many chips are there supposed to be in here? There are a lot of empty niches, and it seems you forgot to mention the exact number."

"How many are there?"

"Two. One white, one red."

Sherman nodded. "That's right."

"And how am I supposed to know if you're telling me the truth?"

"I don't particularly care. Take the chance, Morrison. You're not much of a gambler, but you really should take a chance once in your life."

Morrison nodded. "All right. I have to believe you."

"That's fine. You believe me. But how am I supposed to know whether or not you'll uphold your end of the bargain?"

Bobbi smiled and sat on the arm of Morrison's chair. She put a hand on his shoulder. "You can take my word for that, Sherman. I explained it to you once. Alex and I have discussed the whole thing. All he wants to do is go back to Earth and run his business without your interference."

Sherman laughed. Morrison leaned forward in his chair almost knocking Bobbi off the arm.

"Come on now. What makes you think he told you the truth?" Sherman asked.

Bobbi looked insulted. "He did. I know he did. Tell him, Alex."

"Tell him yourself," Morrison said. "And when you're through, leap out the airlock. I've had it with you. You're as bad as him. You two deserve each other. Maybe I should space the both of you at the same time. Wouldn't that be touching?"

Bobbi's face hardened. She got up off the chair arm and took two quick steps toward Sherman. She wheeled around and pointed the small automatic at Morrison. Morrison chuckled and reached into his pocket, then was struck by the sudden, cold realization that the gun she was pointing was his. But she wouldn't. She couldn't.

"Cute, Bobbi," Morrison said. "Now give me the gun. You can't pull the trigger."

"You're right," she said. "I can't." She threw the gun across to Sherman. "But he can."

Morrison blanched.

Sherman rose to his feet and, pointing the gun straight at Morrison's chest, held out his hand. "The chips?"

Morrison shook his head. "Never."

Sherman shrugged. "Either way. It's okay with

me. You can give them to me and stay alive, or I can kill you and take them."

Morrison shook his head, staring at the deck. "Why?" he asked softly.

"Why, what?" Sherman asked.

"Not you—her. Why'd you do it?"

Bobbi was crying silently. "Because, Alex, I really believed you. You lied to me—you were willing to let all those people die when it would have been so easy to save them. You've always used me, and I guess I'm used to that. But I don't like being used like this."

"Enough," Sherman said. "Lie down on your stomach," he told Morrison.

Morrison eased his bulk out of the chair and lay face down on the deck.

"See if it's still there," Sherman told Bobbi.

She walked over and felt the back of Morrison's neck.

"Well?" Sherman asked.

"I can't tell."

He took a step closer and waved the gun at Morrison's head. "It's got to be there. Look harder." He shifted his weight nervously. "Dig your nails in."

"What are you trying to do?" Morrison demanded.

"Shut up!" Sherman said.

Bobbi felt around for a few more moments, then looked up at Sherman, surprised. "I can feel it!"

"Sit on his back by the shoulder blades. It's probably a plastic graft. Try to peel it off."

She did as Sherman had requested and managed to bare the receptacle that had been hidden for years.

"Now put this in," he said, handing her the red chip.

Bobbi did as she was told.

16

Hello, Alex. Why are you on the floor.

What? Who are you? Morrison thought.

Donald Sherman. Take a few moments to get used to the idea. I'm going to show you what it's like to be a miner, working for you, what those people have to go through, what you've done to them.

Get out of my mind! Leave me alone!

Morrison felt violated in an eerie, discomforting way. It was like nothing he'd ever experienced, but he was powerless, unable to fight Sherman's personality in the red chip.

Images flowed by in his mind, slowly at first, then

with greater speed and clarity. When it was done, Morrison knew what Donald Sherman was all about. He felt weak and very vulerable.

—Hello, Alex, another voice said in his mind.

Morrison looked around the room.

—I said hello. Don't you greet old friends, or haven't you changed that much?

Who is that? Morrison demanded silently.

It's Sherman. You remember me, don't you?

No! It's not the same voice! There are two of you in me! Morrison screamed to himself.

Two of us? Of course there are. There are more than that.

"Help me, Sherman. What's going on? What are you doing to me? I don't understand!" Morrison shouted.

"Sorry," Sherman said, sitting down and crossing his legs. "You're on your own."

"Bobbi?!"

"Like the man said, Alex."

—Where's Helene? the second voice asked.

And then Morrison recognized it. He thought he was going to be sick and had to take a deep breath to control his aching, queasy stomach. The second voice had asked about Helene. Vladimir?

—Yes, it's Vladimir. You killed her.

Oh God. No, Vladimir. Please. I didn't mean to kill her. Let me explain.

—I understand. These things happen. Don't they, Alex? Just like what happened to me, huh? Someone gets a little too powerful, a little too smart for their own good, and you've got to get them out of the way. I understand. These things can't be helped.

Morrison started thrashing about on the floor, trying desperately to rise to his feet. He couldn't control his movements, though, and he flopped around on the deck as if he was having a seizure.

Tell them to leave us alone, Morrison.

Morrison said nothing.

—**Leave him to me.**

"Leave us alone," Morrison said. "Wait outside."

Vladimir? How can you . . . ?

—**Stay out of this, Donald. Don't interfere. I never told you that I existed alongside you in this chip. I waited to show myself.**

—**Alex, you're going to have to do whatever I want you to do. Donald's personality was never strong enough in this red chip to control anyone's motor functions—that was because I needed the space for myself.**

"Leave, will you, please?" Morrison shouted at Bobbi and Sherman.

Why do you want them to leave? Morrison thought. *Why did you make me say that? What are you going to do?*

—**You'll find out, Alex. You'll find out soon enough.**

Sherman and Bobbi left the lounge.

Vladimir made Morrison stand up and walk over to the bar. He rummaged through the bottles until he found what he wanted. Vodka.

But I don't like vodka, Morrison thought.

—**Too bad. You'll just have to get used to it from now on.**

He poured a stiff shot and downed it in one gulp. Morrison gasped for air to Vladimir's chuckles.

—**Okay, Alexander. You've got a choice. A clear, simple, clean-cut choice.**

What? Morrison thought.

—**Lose some weight, act like a human being, run your company like it should be run, or take a walk with me. A walk through the airlock.**

You wouldn't do that.

Morrison started walking toward the door to the lounge.

Stop, Morrison thought. All right. You'd do it.

He wanted to pace, but Vladimir wouldn't let him. He tried to reach up to the back of his neck, but his hand never even moved. Vladimir was controling him like no one had ever done before.

—Well? What's your answer? I'm not going to live in a body like this.

What? Live in my body? Morrison shrieked mentally. If you keep this chip in me it'll kill me! Are you insane?

—Perhaps. Let me show you something.

Morrison's mind was pummeled with images and memories, all through the eyes of a younger Vladimir. Helene was there, young, pretty, happy, and in love. Morrison saw what Vladimir's relationship with Helene had been, the joys and fears of living with a person who cared. Then he started to realize what Vladimir had felt like after she had been taken away, what his life had become without her. The pain, the self-torture, the agony of loneliness, Vladimir's change in attitudes toward Morrison, his inability to get revenge until Sherman had decided to rebel.

—Well? Am I insane, or are you?

Morrison knew better than to think about it. Vladimir would be listening to every thought, every plan for getting the red chip out of his long unused receptacle. If he could have screamed, he would have.

He walked across to the bar and refilled his glass. He took a shaky sip, spilling a little of the clear liquid over his fleshy, stubby fingers. He looked around the lounge, then walked over to the doorway, and peered into the passageway. Bobbi was standing there, talking to Sherman.

"Would you both mind coming inside?" Morrison asked.

Bobbi looked confused. She and Sherman entered the lounge.

Morrison took a deep swallow of vodka. "Well, it's all been settled." He was grinning. "Here are your chips back, Donald."

Morrison screamed out his frustration and agony, but no one heard it but Vladimir. His smile broadened.

Sherman had dropped the gun to his side, forgetting to point it at Morrison. "You're not Morrison—"

"Relax. Let's sit down and I'll tell you all about it."

"Vladimir!" Sherman yelled.

Morrison nodded, and they threw their arms around one another. Bobbi looked on, confused.

"We'll have to get a meditech to cover this receptacle again. Morrison's body may not live long with this chip in it, but at least it will do the things it should have done long ago."

Bobbi shook her head. "I don't understand. What's going on? Will someone explain this to me?"

Morrison laughed.

"Where did you come from, Vladimir? I thought you were dead—"

Morrison smiled, letting his laughter subside slowly. "I was dead. I guess I still am. Are you dead, Donald?"

They both laughed again.

"Will someone tell me what's going on?" Bobbi demanded.

"Sorry," Sherman said. "Let's sit down. We can afford to relax a little, take it easy. We have a lot of work ahead of us."

THE INTEGRATED MAN

The three of them sat down and looked at each other.

"I'm sorry about Helene, Vladimir," Donald said.

Vladimir nodded. "I know. But at least it's over, now."

"Yes," Donald said, nodding. "That it is."

ABOUT THE AUTHOR

MICHAEL BERLYN was born in Brookline, Massachusetts and received a degree in Humanities and Science from Florida Atlantic University. He began writing at the age of fifteen and started concentrating on science fiction in his early twenties. **The Integrated Man** is his second novel, the first being **Crystal Phoenix.** Mr. Berlyn has held a variety of jobs, including pinball arcade money changer, sales manager for a multi-million dollar corporation and electric violin player in a professional rock-and-roll band. For relaxation, Mr. Berlyn enjoys painting watercolors and listening to his vast music collection. His pleasure reading ranges from science texts to mainstream literature to science fiction. He is currently living in West Palm Beach, Florida, with his wife, the author M.M. McClung.

FANTASY AND SCIENCE FICTION FAVORITES

Bantam brings you the recognized classics as well as the current favorites in fantasy and science fiction. Here you will find the beloved Conan books along with recent titles by the most respected authors in the genre.

☐	01166	URSHURAK	
		Bros. Hildebrandt & Nichols	$8.95
☐	13610	NOVA Samuel R. Delany	$2.25
☐	13534	TRITON Samuel R. Delany	$2.50
☐	13612	DHALGREN Samuel R. Delany	$2.95
☐	12018	CONAN THE SWORDSMAN #1	
		DeCamp & Carter	$1.95
☐	12706	CONAN THE LIBERATOR #2	
		DeCamp & Carter	$1.95
☐	12970	THE SWORD OF SKELOS #3	
		Andrew Offutt	$1.95
☐	14321	THE ROAD OF KINGS #4	$2.25
		Karl E. Wagner	
☐	14127	DRAGONSINGER Anne McCaffrey	$2.50
☐	14204	DRAGONSONG Anne McCaffrey	$2.50
☐	12019	KULL Robert E. Howard	$1.95
☐	10779	MAN PLUS Frederik Pohl	$1.95
☐	11736	FATA MORGANA William Kotzwinkle	$2.95
☐	11042	BEFORE THE UNIVERSE	$1.95
		Pohl & Kornbluth	
☐	13680	TIME STORM Gordon R. Dickson	$2.50
☐	13400	SPACE ON MY HANDS Frederic Brown	$1.95